D1331912

'God preserve me from rich men's daughters,' said Gideon North contemptuously. Susan French wasn't rich at all—but she was pretending to be Della Benton, who was; so if and when Gideon discovered the deception, it was hardly going to improve his opinion of her, was it? And why did she care so much?

Books you will enjoy
by MARJORIE LEWTY

LOVE IS A DANGEROUS GAME
Paul Caister was a devastatingly attractive man,
while Kate—well, when he had described her as
'a little grey mouse of a clergyman's daughter'
he wasn't far wrong; certainly she was well out
of her depth with him. So what was she doing
in Hong Kong, pretending to be his fiancée?

PRISONER IN PARADISE
Being stranded in Mexico at the tender age of
eighteen, with no money, no friends, and no
job, was a thoroughly unpleasant experience,
Sara found, and she would have been grateful
to anyone who got her out of it. But her rescuer
had to be the formidable Jason Knight, who
made no secret of his low opinion of her. She
had to get away from him—but how?

A CERTAIN SMILE
To discover her father for the first time at the
age of eighteen was an overwhelming experience for Amanda. She was whisked from a
quiet Devon village into a world of wealth, of
tycoons, of sophistication—and a world that
also contained Blair Craddock. Wasn't it all
going to be too much for her?

A VERY SPECIAL MAN
It would take a very special man indeed to
make Chloe fall in love again, after Roger. So
it was not because she had considered him
'special' that after all Chloe had married Benedict Dane, but so that he could put his
grandmother's mind at rest. And to conceal the
affair he was having with a beautiful Spanish
girl—as Chloe discovered when, far too late,
she realised she had fallen in love with Benedict
after all . . .

BEYOND
THE LAGOON

BY

MARJORIE LEWTY

MILLS & BOON LIMITED

15–16 BROOK'S MEWS
LONDON W1A 1DR

All the characters in this book have no existence out-side the imagination of the Author, and have no re-lation whatsoever to anyone bearing the same name or names. They are not even distantly inspired by any individual known or unknown to the Author, and all the incidents are pure invention.

The text of this publication or any part thereof may not be reproduced or transmitted in any form or by any means, electronic or mechanical, including photo-copying, recording, storage in an information retrieval system, or otherwise, without the written permission of the publisher.

This book is sold subject to the condition that it shall not, by way of trade or otherwise, be lent, resold, hired out or otherwise circulated without the prior consent of the publisher in any form of binding or cover other than that in which it is published and without a similar condition including this condition being imposed on the subsequent purchaser.

First published 1981
Australian copyright 1981
Philippine copyright 1981
This edition 1981

© Marjorie Lewty 1981

ISBN 0 263 73589 3

Set in 10 on 11½ pt. Monophoto Times

*Made and printed in Great Britain by
Richard Clay (The Chaucer Press) Ltd.,
Bungay, Suffolk*

CHAPTER ONE

'No.' Susan French shook her fair head decisively. 'I'm sorry, Mr Benton, but I can't do what you ask.'

Her eyes, large and velvet brown and very direct, met the angry eyes of the man on the opposite side of the wide desk, and for a moment her nerve faltered as his heavy face slowly turned crimson and the bushy brows drew together over pale eyes that seemed to send out shafts of pure, vibrating anger. Nobody ever dared to say no to John Benton, chairman of Benton's Enterprises. At least, nobody had dared for a very long time. Until now.

'Can't?' he roared. 'What do you mean, girl, you can't do it? Of course you can. You'll do exactly as I say. No problem. You'll come along with me now to see Carter, and you'll explain to him that the mistake was yours about leaving out that clause.'

'But it wasn't——' Susan began.

He went on as if she hadn't spoken. 'You can say that I was away that day and that you shouldn't have sent it off without my seeing it, but you knew he was waiting for it. The blasted fellow has more or less accused me of trying to pull a fast one on him, but that way he'll believe it was simply your error.' The angry eyes probed Susan's oval face with its tenderly-shaped mouth, its luminous brown eyes under long lashes, beneath smooth, lint-fair hair that was taken back demurely and tied with a black bow. 'You look as if butter wouldn't melt in your mouth,' he added sourly.

'If you play your cards right, like I say, Carter's bound to be convinced.'

Susan's smooth brow wrinkled. 'But the mistake wasn't mine, Mr Benton. You told me yourself to miss out that clause in the contract. You said Mr Carter knew it was being deleted. And you did see the contract before it was sent off, so how can I say you didn't?'

The man opposite heaved a gusty breath and looked up at the ceiling and then down at Susan, who was beginning to feel that she was getting smaller and smaller every minute. 'Good God, girl, do you *have* to be so dense? I'm running a business, not a Sunday School outing.' His voice changed, became placating and slightly wheedling. 'You want to get on, don't you, Susan? When they shifted you up to be my secretary you told me you were ambitious. Well now, here's your chance. You just do as I want and I'll see you don't lose by it. You know how important this contract with Carter's is to me—to our company?'

'Yes,' said Susan.

'The biggest this year—the biggest ever, for that matter. Well now, doesn't your sense of loyalty mean anything to you? Loyalty to the company—to me?'

'Yes, of course it does, Mr Benton,' said Susan unhappily. 'But I can't do what you ask. It would be a—a cover-up, wouldn't it? We trick Carter's by leaving out that clause, hoping it will get past them like that, and then make a lot more money on the contract than we would have done otherwise.'

John Benton's grin was like a gash across his heavy face. 'Clever girl, Susan! We need girls with intelligence in the company—you'll go far.' He got to his feet. 'Come along then, let's go and see Carter straight away. He's expecting me at eleven.'

Susan remained seated. He was rushing her now—bulldozing her into doing something that her conscience revolted against. She felt cold and trembly. She was aware that this was a crisis, but she had taken a stand and she couldn't change her mind.

She shook her head. 'I'm sorry, but I'm not coming, Mr Benton.'

He stood glaring down at her and she fixed her gaze miserably on the desk in front of her. John Benton was a big man, over six feet and broad with it. Flabby and out of condition though he was, his mere physical presence beside her was alarming. He drew in a rasping breath. 'You mean to disobey me?'

'I'm afraid so,' whispered Susan.

There was a horrid silence as it finally dawned on John Benton that he wasn't going to get his own way. Then his huge hand came down on the desk with a thud. 'You stupid, idiotic bitch! Why the blazes did they give me a goody-goody little fool for a secretary? All right then, if you won't you won't, I'll have to find someone who will.' He spat out the words, furious now, his face purpling. He looked as if he would like to do her bodily injury. 'Get out and stay out!' he shouted. 'From this moment you're sacked! Get your things now, this minute, and go, and don't let me set eyes on you again, blast you, or I won't be responsible for my actions!'

Susan was on her feet now, gripping the edge of the desk, her knees like rubber and her palms clammy. John Benton strode past, then stopped abruptly as the door opened. Through the impotent tears that hazed her eyes Susan saw the figure of Della, Mr Benton's young daughter, standing in the doorway.

'Della! What the blazes are you doing here? Who said

you could walk in just like that? I've told you never to interrupt me at the office.' The angry voice hadn't softened at all.

'I had to have a word with you, Daddy. It's terribly urgent. *Please!*' It was impossible to miss the desperate note in the girl's voice, but nothing was going to stop her father now.

'Then it'll bloody well have to wait,' he told her roughly, on his way through the open doorway.

'But I must talk to you now, Daddy, there's something——' She grabbed his arm.

He shook off her hand. 'You heard what I said, Della, *not now*. Don't you understand?' The violence of his temper, running wild, exploded through the office. 'Get back home and don't come pestering me.'

He brushed past her and strode into the outer office, where his voice boomed on. Susan couldn't hear the words, but she knew the tone well enough to recognise that he was issuing curt instructions. Then the outside door slammed and there was silence.

The two girls looked at each other, helpless and embarrassed. Then Della Benton sank into the big chair her father had vacated and said shakily, 'Crikey, he *is* in a mood!'

Susan pursed her lips. 'You can say that again.'

Her own desk was at the far end of the big office. She went over to it and began to open drawers, collecting her personal belongings. She couldn't get out of this place fast enough.

It hadn't lasted long, this job that was going to be so wonderful. When she had been promoted, two months ago, to take the place of the secretary who was on leave recovering from an operation, she couldn't believe her luck. But that was before she found out what working for John Benton, the chairman, was like. Her secretarial training had warned her that working for a top man might be tough and she had been prepared. She had long ago learned to stand on her own two feet—being brought up by an unpractical, though lovable, artist father had taught her that—and she had ambitions to prove herself a good secretary. So she had put up with John Benton's bluster and tempers, his domineering ways, his unreasonable demands on her time and patience. She had even made excuses for him. He was getting to the age when men who live at a high tension begin to show signs of wear and tear.

She tossed a comb and a bundle of her own pens and pencils into her handbag and snapped the clasp. Oh well, it wasn't the end of the world, she could probably get another job, although without a reference (and she certainly wouldn't get one) she'd have to start right from the bottom again. That meant goodbye to her plans to get out of the hostel into a shared flat; perhaps to save enough for a holiday in the sun next year.

She sighed, closing the drawers, leaving the desk tidy. In a way she had enjoyed the work, enjoyed the challenge, but nothing was going to make her agree to take part in a dishonest trick. If that was big business then she preferred to stay in the typing pool and know nothing about it. She was getting over the shock of John Benton's aggressive anger now, her knees had stopped trembling and her eyes were clear. She would go down and collect her cards and the salary owing—presumably she would be paid in lieu of notice; John Benton wouldn't want to go into the reason for sacking her— then she would queue up at a Wimpy's for a coffee and a hamburger before she went to the employment agency in Oxford Street.

She turned to leave the office and then she saw that Della Benton was still there. She was huddled up in the big chair, her beautiful shortie mink coat pulled round her, looking like a forlorn little rabbit, and she was sobbing silently.

Susan hesitated. It was tough luck on any girl to have a father like John Benton—even if it *did* rate mink coats and luxury living—but Della Benton's problems couldn't have anything to do with her, and her first impulse was to walk out and leave her to sort them out herself. But something in the droop of the fair head with its modish haircut, in the sheer abandonment to misery, stopped Susan on her way to the door.

She shrugged, half irritated by her own inability to refrain from offering help when help seemed needed, and went over and stood before the big office chair with its crushed bundle of wretchedness.

She put a hand lightly on the mink-clad shoulder and her fingers sank into the deep softness of the fur. 'It can't be that bad, you know,' she said. 'Nothing's that bad. You get over it.'

That was a lie—before the words were out she knew it. It was two years since Daddy died and the wound seemed just as raw as ever. The memory of him deepened her sympathy for Della Benton, with a father like hers.

A small face raised itself slowly, great dark eyes swimming, their lids red and puffy, pale gold hair clinging damply to a white brow. 'It *is* that bad,' she gulped, and blurted out with a desperate petulance, 'How could you possibly know?' She hiccuped slightly and fumbled for a handkerchief.

Susan gave her a clean one from her handbag. 'I don't know anything about it,' she said crisply. How did one explain an often inconvenient urge to help, without appearing a sentimental do-gooder? 'But as we seem to be fellow-sufferers I thought I might at least offer a shoulder to weep on. Keep the hankie,' she added, turning to the door again.

'Please—please don't go away.' It was a whisper, agonised, pleading. 'Wh-what do you mean—fellow-sufferers?'

Susan paused and then came slowly back again. 'Merely that your father has just torn a large strip off me too,' she said. 'In fact, he's given me the sack—just like that. I'm afraid I made him very angry and that's probably why he didn't exactly seem pleased to see you. You came in for the fag-end of his wrath. I'm sorry, but it wasn't exactly my fault.'

Della wiped her eyes and said haltingly, 'He's sacked you? But—but why? You've always seemed so—so awfully efficient and—and sort of cool and collected when I've seen you.' She sniffed and blew her nose. 'Like—like I wish *I* was.'

'We had a—slight difference of opinion,' Susan said wryly. 'He couldn't get me to change my mind.'

Della regarded her with frank admiration. 'I think that's marvellous. To be able to stand up to my father when he's in a temper—I just don't know how you could do it.'

Susan shrugged. 'It's lost me my job.'

'What will you do now?'

'Have a coffee and a hamburger and then go and look for another job.'

Della had been trying to repair the ravages caused by her tears. Now she snapped the clasp of her make-up bag and said, 'Look, you said we were fellow-sufferers. Come and have some lunch with me and—and let's talk. We could go to my club, it's quiet there.' She looked up at Susan rather shyly. 'Will you?'

Susan saw a girl appealing for help. A girl of her own age, a little like her, in fact, in appearance although in nothing else. A rich man's daughter who wore fabulous clothes and belonged to her own club and whose diamond-studded wrist-watch alone must have cost as much as Susan's salary for six months. Common sense warned her that it would be wiser not to tangle with someone so far outside her own world.

'Please.' Della made a little gesture with her hands towards Susan. A pleading gesture.

'Thank you, I'd like to come,' Susan said, making a decision that was to change her whole life.

The London streets were crowded, as usual, but eventually they managed to get a taxi, which deposited them outside an old-fashioned house in West Kensington.

'My club,' Della announced, leading the way up stone steps and into an entrance hall, carpeted in crimson. A kind of hush lay over it and the winter light that filtered through the long, stained-glass windows added to the sombre atmosphere of the place. 'Trendy, isn't it?' whispered Della with deep sarcasm. 'Father chose it for me—wouldn't you guess? He thinks I'm *safe* here.'

Two grey-haired women in tailored suits passed by. The words of the taller, thinner one cut through the silence. 'My dear Eleanor, if you put your trust in statistics I'm afraid you're going to find yourself extremely vulnerable. As I said to the Under-Secretary yesterday . . .' They marched on and disappeared.

'See what I mean?' Della rolled her eyes upwards. 'Such suitable companions to keep me out of mischief!'

Susan did see. And later, in the half-filled dining room, the impression was even clearer. There couldn't have been a woman there under forty. Some were smart, some expensively dowdy. The majority looked like professional women, but there was a smattering of country types, probably up in Town for a day's shopping. Not one of them looked remotely likely to be in sympathy with Della Benton.

The lunch was hearty and simple—roast beef, Yorkshire pudding and vegetables, followed by apple tart and cream. A conventional lunch for a cold December day, well cooked and a distinct improvement on a hamburger in a crowded Wimpy's, Susan decided, settling down to enjoy it.

Della, on the other hand, wasn't enjoying it at all. She pushed the food around on her plate and left half of it uneaten. She made an effort at small talk, but she was obviously tense and nervous and there were long silences. Susan began to wonder why the girl had invited her at all.

Then, as they sat on a velvet sofa in a mausoleum of a lounge, drinking coffee, Della burst out, 'I don't know what I'm going to do—I feel desperate!' The soft eyes had a wild, hunted look.

'Want to talk about it?' Susan enquired calmly.

It came surging out then. Della sat forward, lacing her fingers, the diamonds in her wrist-watch glinting in the light from the ornate crystal chandelier over their heads.

It was a man, of course. His name was Vic and he was a singer in a pop group—his own group. He was the most wonderful man in the world and Della was in love with him. Not just crazy for him, but *really* in love, she added, her eyes huge and sober, expecting Susan to understand.

'I think I'd die for him,' she said extravagantly. 'You know.'

Susan didn't really know; she'd never felt like that about a man. Some day, perhaps——— 'Does he feel the same way?' she asked.

'Yes—oh yes. He wants us to get married.'

'Well, what's the problem?' Susan prompted. She thought she could guess, but Della looked dreamy, as if she was likely to trail off into silence once more.

The big dark eyes focused on her and then narrowed. 'Wouldn't you know? My father's stopping us. Vic is sort of old-fashioned about some things. He thought we ought to get my father's consent. He went to see him, to sort of lay his cards on the table—prospects and so on——'

'That's nice,' said Susan.

Della's face was suddenly bitter. 'It was daft—I told him, but he wouldn't listen. My father worked himself into a flaming rage and practically threw Vic out. His daughter wasn't going to marry a so-and-so pop singer—you can imagine. But that wasn't what made him mad, really. It was because—he said—I'd gone behind his back and deceived him. When Vic had left he got into a most frightful rage with me.' Her lip quivered. 'I can't stand it when he gets angry. It—it frightens me.'

Susan nodded. 'Yes, I know what you mean. But surely—you're over age, aren't you?'

'I'm twenty.'

'So am I,' said Susan, and smiled. She felt years older than this unhappy girl sitting beside her. 'Well then, you can please yourself. Victorian-type fathers are out of date these days.'

Della said, 'Are they? That's what you think. How would *you* like a father like mine?'

Susan's stomach contracted as if she were warding off a blow. Even after all this time the agony could strike quickly if she wasn't prepared, like a knife slipping between her ribs.

It must have shown in her face, for Della said quickly, 'Oh, I'm sorry. Is he——?'

Susan's mouth was stiff as she tried to smile. 'It's okay, just a reflex thing. He died two years ago, but sometimes it just—hits me. But we were talking about you.'

'About my father, actually, and you know what he's like, don't you? All he's interested in is power—power, and the money that provides it. Oh, he's generous enough, he gives me all I need, but he wields the big stick too. He says what I can do and where I can go and who my friends are, and if there's anything he doesn't approve of he—it's——' She bit her lip and her eyes showed fear. 'I've planned over and over again to walk out, but—I dunno—when it comes to it it doesn't seem as easy as that. I guess I need backbone. I must take after my mother—she couldn't ever stand up to him either. She died when I was fourteen, and now he only has me to bully and it's that much worse.'

She was silent for so long that Susan put in gently, 'What are you going to do now, then? This is something different, isn't it—you'll have to make up your mind.'

'I know. I *had* made up my mind when I came into the office just now. I'd screwed my courage up to tell him I was leaving and going to Vic. I thought if I told him in the office and then just—went—he wouldn't be able to stop me, like he would at home. But——' she shrugged hopelessly '—you saw what happened.' After a moment she went on, 'The worst thing is now that he's arranged to send me off to visit my godfather in the West Indies. It's supposed to be a lovely holiday in the sun for me—and as far as possible from Vic, of course. That's what he thinks. He doesn't know that Vic and his group are starting a tour in the U.S. at the same time. Vic wants me to go along with them—to see how I like the life and everything—but it's hopeless really. If I don't turn up when my godfather is expecting me he'll contact my father and I'll have all the private detectives in London on my trail. My father will be on the next flight and I'll be dragged back home and there'll be frightful scenes.' She shook her head despairingly. 'I couldn't face it.'

Susan drank her coffee and regarded the girl beside her with a mixture of sympathy and irritation. The prospect of a holiday in the sunshine of the West Indies, out of the damp, depressing chill of London in December seemed to her like a glimpse of heaven. Still, she supposed that if going there meant being parted from the man you were desperately in love with, it was understandable that Della should toss it aside as unimportant.

'Yes, I see your difficulty,' she said. 'It's tough.' It was a pity that all she could offer was sympathy. What Della Benton really needed was someone to put a firecracker under her and spur her into action. The first step was always the hardest, and she had obviously been conditioned to a meek submission by a lifetime of domestic tyranny in a household dominated by her abominable father. 'I wish I could help, or suggest something, I really do.'

Della smiled wryly. 'We ought to change places, shouldn't we? If I could manage to stand up to my father like you did, it would be simple.'

'It cost me my job,' said Susan again.

Della nodded. 'Yes. Does it mean a lot to you?'

'I was saving up for a holiday in the sun.' She grinned. 'Spain, most likely. Nothing as expensive and glamorous as the West Indies.'

Della said glumly, 'You can keep the West Indies for me, and all the sun and the sea and the palm trees. I only want to go with Vic.' Suddenly she showed a spark of spirit. She beat her hand on the arm of the sofa. 'Oh, damn, damn, damn! If only there was some way!'

An elderly steward approached. 'There's a gentleman waiting in the hall to see you, Miss Benton.' He ambled gently away.

Della had gone white. 'Vic!' she breathed. 'It must be Vic. I told him not to come here.' She jumped to her feet, tossing the mink jacket round her shoulders, and hurried across the lounge.

Susan followed more slowly. She would give Della and her boy-friend time to meet, and then take her leave. She had done what she could to help, which wasn't much, but they wouldn't want her with them now.

She found Della standing beside an enormous rubber plant, glancing furtively round as if its giant leaves could conceal her. Beside her stood a tall, fair, slim young man with humorous eyes.

Susan hesitated, but Della motioned to her to join them. 'Susan, this is Vic.' She spoke his name with a kind of warm ecstasy. 'Vic darling, this is Susan—she's my father's secretary.'

'Was,' corrected Susan.

Della grimaced. '*Was.* We've both fallen foul of my father's temper this morning, Vic, only poor Susan has lost her job. We've been lunching together and wiping the tears from each other's eyes.' She laughed. She was full of life and vitality now, with Vic beside her, but it was too brittle, too high-strung.

Susan's hand was taken in a firm grasp while a pair of crinkly blue eyes smiled into hers. He wasn't handsome, this man of Della's, but he had the kind of bony, interesting, crooked face that would send the fans wild.

'Hullo, Susan,' he said, and then, staring harder, 'Good lord!'

'What's the matter, Vic? Have you and Susan met before?' Della was on her guard immediately with the quick wariness of a girl in love.

Vic shook his head, still looking incredulous. 'Never,' he said. 'Have we, Susan?'

'No, never,' confirmed Susan, wondering what all this was about. 'Well, I'll be on my way. Thank you for the lunch, Miss Benton, I enjoyed it very much.'

'Thank you for coming.' Della was polite, but vague now, her eyes only for the man beside her. 'I hope you find another job soon.'

Susan smiled, nodded to Vic and walked briskly out of the building. Poor Della, she thought, as she waited for a bus to take her back to Oxford Street. How absolutely wretched to be saddled with a father like John Benton for the rest of your life! Would her love for Vic be strong enough to overcome her fear of her father? Susan hoped so. She had liked the look of the young singer; he looked responsible and dependable, and very much in love. She wondered how it would all work out, but she would probably never know. Unless Vic got to the top and she saw their photographs together in a magazine. That would be satisfying, and it would be nice to think that John Benton had been taken down a few pegs. He deserved it.

Her bus swept up and she climbed to the upper deck,

putting Della Benton's problems out of her mind and beginning to concentrate on her own.

By seven o'clock that evening the difficulties seemed to have multiplied and grown into a thick fog, through which she couldn't see her way. Everything seemed dull and dreary, including the sitting room at the hostel. She sat in one of the brown chairs—the one with a broken spring—and tried to interest herself in a magazine, until it was time to go to bed.

She had spent an unsatisfactory afternoon trailing round the agencies in the rain, trying to explain why she couldn't produce a reference, and had ended up with three 'possibles' for tomorrow, none of them sounding interesting and all in the lowest-paid bracket.

She had had a coffee and a sandwich in Oxford Street—more to get inside out of the cold of the December day than because she felt hungry—and then had come back to the hostel in Bayswater, feeling more depressed than she could remember feeling for a long time.

All the other women residents of the hostel were out—all except Serinder, poring over her textbooks in the far corner of the big room, her patterned sari pulled round her feet, her beautiful dark eyes intent. She had come to England to get an education and she was dedicated to getting one.

Susan wished desperately that *she* were dedicated to something. Some future that held out meaning and satisfaction. Perhaps when Daddy died she should have stayed on another year at school and tried for a university place and a grant, which had been her original plan. But the solicitor, who was the only person she could turn to for advice, had suggested that it might be better to take what little money there was from the insurance policy, and get herself a secretarial training, and that was what she had done. Just then she didn't care what she did; she didn't care about anything for a long time, and learning shorthand and typing and audio work, living at the reasonably inexpensive hostel, had filled in that first awful, blank year after she found herself quite alone in the world.

Later she got her first job in an insurance office. When that didn't hold out much prospect of advancement, she thought herself lucky to get taken on at Benton's Enterprises. The work was more varied and she had begun to come back to life again, feeling a spark of ambition to become a really top secretary. She had worked hard, made a few friends, dated once or twice with boys from the office, who had a habit of cooling off when they found she lived in a hostel and was expected to be in at a reasonable time at night. She didn't mind. None of them promised to fill any gap in her life and she didn't at all enjoy the parties they took her to.

Then she had been taken out of the typing pool to be John Benton's secretary, when his own secretary was ill. And look how *that* had ended!

She was a misfit in London, she decided now, wishing that Daddy had never decided to come here, just because it was possible to get some part-time art teaching to boost the small income he made from selling his pictures.

'I want to be able to give you more, Susan love,' he had said. 'Pretty clothes, and all the things a young lady needs.'

She let the magazine drop to her lap, remembering him and his care and love for her; his unworldly attitude to most things, including money; his delicate, intricate little pictures of flowers and animals and living things that had sold well enough to keep them when they lived in the country. Yes, coming to London had been a dreadful mistake, a mistake for both of them. If they had stayed in their Devon cottage Daddy wouldn't have been walking along the Edgware Road on that dark wet night two years ago, when a lorry skidded and——

Susan still shuddered when she remembered it.

A sudden resolve came to her. She would get away, get out of London and carve a new life for herself somewhere where she wouldn't be likely to work for men like John Benton, she thought with distaste. She never wanted to encounter a man like that again.

The telephone rang in the hall. Susan waited a moment to see if the housekeeper was going to answer it, and when it went on ringing she got up and went out herself.

A man's voice queried the number. Then, 'May I speak to Miss Susan French, please, if she's in?'

'This is Susan French speaking.' Puzzling! She didn't recognise the voice.

'Oh great! Susan, this is Vic—Vic Wild. We met this morning at Della's club, remember? Look, are you terribly busy?'

She glanced through the open door into the dreary sitting room. 'Well, not really.'

'That's fine.' The voice tingled with excitement. 'Look, something's come up and I'd like to talk to you. I'm ringing from a callbox just round the corner from you. I'll be with you in a couple of minutes, okay?'

'Well——' Susan began, baffled.

'See you,' said Vic, and rang off.

She replaced the receiver and stood looking at it

thoughtfully, and almost at once the front door bell rang. She opened it and Vic stood there.

'Della's waiting at my place,' he said hastily. 'She hasn't got much time because she's supposed to be meeting her father for dinner at eight o'clock. He keeps tabs on her all the time, the miserable old so-and-so. But we've come up with a brilliant idea and we want to talk to you about it. Will you come? I've got a taxi waiting outside.'

Susan stared at him for a moment, then something of his own eagerness touched her. She had longed for something interesting to happen, hadn't she? 'Just wait till I get my coat,' she said.

The taxi dived into the traffic, lurching along darkened streets and round corners until Susan was completely lost. 'How did you know where I lived?' she asked Vic.

'Easy—Della rang up the office. That was the least of our problems.' He didn't volunteer any more information and sat on the edge of his seat as if he could help the taxi along. When it stopped outside a tall old house in a quiet, shabby square, he leaped out, paid the driver, and grabbed Susan's arm, leading her up a bare staircase to the top floor.

He threw open a door and announced in triumph, 'Here she is—I've got her!'

Susan found herself in a large room, furnished scantily and extremely untidy. There was an upright piano at one end, and complex-looking audio equipment beside it. Posters covered the walls, and magazines and cushions were strewn around the floor. There was a low table with a coffee percolator, and mugs, and milk in a bottle. A three-bar electric fire threw a warm glow over the whole room.

Della Benton was alone in the room, and she jumped up from a pouffe by the fire. 'Marvellous! Thanks for coming, Susan, you're an angel.' Her big dark eyes were shining with an excitement that matched Vic's, only Susan thought she saw apprehension in her face, while Vic seemed sublimely confident.

'Now, girls, let's get comfortable and then we can talk.'

Della handed round coffee and Susan sat on the pouffe while the other two seated themselves very close together on a small sofa. They looked rather an oddly-assorted pair, Susan thought—Della in an exquisite silky two-piece in pastel pink with a choker of small pearls that were probably real, and her diamond-studded wrist-watch, and her high-heeled fashion shoes that breathed Italy, Vic in his old jeans and cotton safari jacket, his soft fair hair flopping over his bony forehead. But the love that was between them went far beyond any surface differences. It was like a flame that lit up the whole studio. Susan found herself longing to help them. She was sure that was why they had brought her here, although she hadn't a clue how she could do it. She waited for Vic to explain.

But for once the irrepressible Vic seemed at a loss how to begin. He drank his coffee, sat in silence for a while and then, drawing Della close with one long, bony arm, he said seriously, 'Susan, this is going to sound scatty, but don't say anything until you've heard it all. Della's told you that her father's sending her away to her godfather on an island in the Caribbean, to get her away from me? Well, I don't intend to let that happen if there's any way I can stop it—any way at all, however much of a gamble it may seem. What I want is to take her along with me and my group on a tour we're doing in the U.S. and Mexico. I want Della to have a chance to see if she thinks she can put up with the crazy life of being married to a singer.'

'Vic darling, you *know*——' Della interrupted, but he stopped her words with a kiss.

'Yes, I know, sweetheart, but you've got to be sure. It wouldn't be fair to you otherwise. If I thought it would, I'd drag you off and marry you tomorrow, father or no father.' The look he gave the girl beside him as he drew her close made Susan think how wonderful it would be to have a man so much in love with you.

Vic looked back at Susan. 'It wouldn't be any good to try to persuade Della just to break away and come with us, because it's certain her father would find out where we were and come after her and all hell would be let loose. She's had about enough already—she couldn't take that. So——' he paused and for the first time he seemed anxious '—so we'll have to resort to beating Mr John Benton at his own game. A spot of trickery, I mean. Something he's very good at himself.'

Susan nodded. She knew all about John Benton and his tricks. She hoped quite fiercely that Vic and Della would succeed. John Benton deserved everything that was coming to him. 'Good luck to you,' she said. 'I hope you pull it off. How can I help?'

'I was coming to that.' There was a faint awkwardness in Vic's voice now. 'It really all depends on you, Susan. You see, a sort of vague plan began to form in my mind the moment I saw you and Della together. It shook me rigid—the likeness between you two. You might have been twins. Didn't you notice it yourself, Susan?'

Susan shook her head. 'No, I—I always thought Della was awfully pretty, so I wouldn't imagine——'

She looked at the girl on the sofa in a bewildered sort of way. 'I—I suppose we're the same colouring, the same brown eyes, the same sort of size, but——'

Vic stood up, grabbed both girls by the hand, and led them over to a large mirror that hung on the wall, a huge Victorian affair in a gilt frame. 'Look!' he said triumphantly.

Susan looked doubtfully at her reflection, then at Della's, then back again. 'Ye-es, I suppose so,' she said.

A mischievous smile played round Della's mouth. 'Let your hair loose,' she said, reaching up to untie the ribbon, and Susan's silky gold hair fell forward over her ears, curving to her shoulders, just as Della's did. 'See?'

'Yes, I see.' Susan began to laugh. 'It's extraordinary.'

Vic was grinning widely as they went back to their seats beside the fire. 'That's what put it into my mind,' he said. 'I thought to myself, "If only this girl could go out to the Cayman Islands instead of Della, so Della could come with me!" It seemed a mad notion, but then Della told me about how her father had behaved to you, Susan, and how he'd put you out of a job, and how you couldn't have any tender feelings towards him, and then I began to turn it over in my mind and that's when I came up with my plan.'

Susan's heart sank as she thought she saw what they were going to ask her to do. 'Just a minute,' she put in quickly. 'If you were thinking of asking me to take Della's place—to try to impersonate her—I'm afraid it's not on. I simply couldn't do it.'

Della shook her head vigorously and Vic said, 'No, you've got it all wrong, it's not like that. Anyway, Della is a great favourite with her godfather, and he wouldn't be taken in for a moment. No, this is our plan, and it's

quite innocent. Della is booked to fly out to the Caymans, changing planes at Miami, on Tuesday, and her
father will be at the airport to make jolly sure she goes.
Now we—the boys and I—are starting out on a tour of
Florida and Mexico, and I fixed it that we should travel
on the same day, only on an earlier plane, a charter
flight to Miami. I booked an extra seat in case Della
would come with us. If you travelled with us, Susan—
no, don't say anything yet, let me finish—if you travelled to Miami with us then we could wait until Della's
plane arrived there, and effect a change-over. Della
could come with me and you could go on to the Caymans on her ticket. Once there, you could see her godfather and explain how things are, do your best to win
him over to our cause. Ask him to give us a few days, a
week, even, and then it could all be tidied up. We're not
asking you to do anything dishonest, and we would
promise to keep in close touch by phone to see how
things are going. If Della's godfather is open to reason,
then you'd have a lovely few days basking in the sun in
the Caribbean. And if he won't play, then we'd come
along straight away and take over from you. What do
you say?'

Susan stared into a pair of bright blue eyes with
laughter lines at the corners. But Vic wasn't laughing
now; he looked as if he was pleading for his life. 'It's
crazy,' she gasped. 'You're both crazy!'

Della and Vic looked at each other, their hands
clasped. 'I guess we are,' said Vic. 'Two crazy people.'
He bent and laid his cheek against Della's and her eyes
filled with tears.

Oh lord, Susan thought, it's going to be hard to
refuse to help these two. 'But there'd be so much to
arrange, so many things to think about.'

She saw the look that passed between the two on the sofa. They knew she was weakening.

'Only two things really,' Vic urged. 'First, do you have a passport? You wouldn't need one for the Caymans—it's a British colony—but if you're travelling to Miami with us it would be safer to have one.'

Susan nodded. 'I got one only a few weeks ago. Mr Benton's going to a conference in Germany and he was going to take me with him.'

'That's okay, then. The second thing is a bit more delicate.' Vic grinned tentatively. 'Is there anyone to consult? Anyone who'd object?'

'Do I have a boy-friend, you mean?' She smiled back at him, shaking her head. 'My soulmate doesn't seem to have turned up yet.'

Della's eyes twinkled with mischief. 'Have a look round the Caymans, then. You might find what you're looking for. By the way, I ought to warn you, there's a bloke out there called North—Gideon North—that my father's got all lined up for me. He's something in one of the big financial companies there and he's a friend of Uncle Ben's. The Cayman Islands are a super tax haven, by the way. There's no income tax, or something. I don't really understand it, but that's why Uncle Ben settled there when he retired a few years ago. He's rolling in money, and I suppose this North man is too. That's why my darling father has been trying to sell me the idea of capturing him.' She pulled a disgusted face.

Vic chuckled. 'I'll be rolling in money too, one of these days soon. Wait until we get into the charts!'

Della reached up and kissed him. 'Don't be silly—I'd rather have you on twopence a week than any iron-jawed, middle-aged financial wizard.'

Susan entered into the joke. 'I'm not sure Gideon

what's-his-name sounds like my dreamboat either.'

'Don't worry,' Della assured her. 'When he finds out you're not John Benton's little girl he'll be off and away. Money goes for money, all along their financial line, and don't I know it? It's all they think about—except for Uncle Ben, that is. He's a sweetie and he can't help being stinking rich.'

They all laughed. Then, suddenly, they were all silent.

Della's dark eyes were very large and solemn. 'Will you help us, Susan dear? We've got an awful nerve to ask you, but—but you did say we were fellow-sufferers, didn't you?'

A picture of John Benton, raging and roaring and bullying and scheming, using everybody as things to be manipulated and tyrannised over, came clearly into Susan's mind. Then she looked at his daughter, who wasn't quite tough enough to stand up to him.

If ever a nice girl needed a helping hand it was Della Benton.

She pulled a wry face. 'I think we must all be mad,' she said. 'But I'll have a go.'

CHAPTER TWO

EVERYTHING had gone so smoothly it was almost too good to be true. Susan stood beside her luggage—or rather, Della's luggage—in the arrivals lounge at Grand Cayman airport and looked around for the man who was supposed to be meeting her.

Sixtyish and plump, with a pink face and a neat white beard—that was how Della had described her godfather Uncle Ben Caldicott, who was her mother's uncle. 'He's a poppet, that's why I don't mind asking you to tackle him. I'm almost sure he'll understand and back us up.'

The lounge was full; mostly, it seemed, with tourists from the U.S., talking twenty-nine to the dozen, preparing to wring every second of enjoyment out of their stay in the island paradise. But not a white beard in sight.

Della sat down and waited, scanning every new face that passed. Uncle Ben Caldicott couldn't be expected to recognise her—she wasn't Della, even if she did look absurdly like her—and she would have to contact him as soon as she saw him. She had her spiel all ready. 'Mr Caldicott?' she would say. 'I'm Susan French, a friend of Della Benton's. I hope it isn't too much of a shock to see me turning up instead of Della, but if we could go somewhere to talk I could explain why she's asked me to come.'

Then, with any luck, he would take her to his house, or apartment, or whatever, and she would be able to tell him the whole story. She wished he would hurry up, she was beginning to get butterflies inside now. What if Della had misjudged him and if he were really angry? She was going to have to convince him that what Della and Vic felt for each other was the real thing. And it wasn't as if Della was a child. She was over twenty, a grown woman and perfectly entitled to make up her own mind what she would do and whom she would marry.

Any doubts that Susan herself might have still entertained had been finally dispelled when Della's plane arrived in Miami and she saw the look on her face just before she threw herself into Vic's arms. He had looked kind of dazed too, as if he couldn't quite believe his luck.

Susan had enjoyed the flight from Heathrow yesterday. It was her first time in a plane and she had taken to it from the moment the huge jet lifted its nose and soared into the sky above London. It was like magic to see the great buildings shrinking into a toy city; then the green of the downs merging into rocks and sea as they crossed the coastline and finally there were only white clouds below, parting now and then to show the deep blue of endless ocean.

Vic and the three other young men of his group had been vastly amused at her ecstatic reaction. They had laughed at her and teased her. They were—or liked to think they were—all seasoned jet travellers. But to Susan it was all new and exciting and she saw no reason to pretend to be bored and blasé. She had agreed to take on this assignment and she was going to have as much enjoyment as she could get out of it.

The changeover at Miami airport had been effected without a hitch. Susan and Vic had been waiting in the transit lounge when Della arrived. They had all been a little tensed up, as if John Benton was suddenly going to appear and snatch Della away, but of course no such thing happened.

Della handed over her return ticket to Susan. 'The Cayman Islands apparently insist on a return ticket, in case you like the place so much you might stay for ever,' she grinned. 'Anyway, there it is, and you'll know you can always fly back to London if by any remote chance things get too sticky. It's got my name on it, but I'm sure nobody's going to bother about that. You'll have to pick up my luggage when you arrive, and I hope you'll like the stuff I've packed. We're both size ten, aren't we, so it should fit okay. There are two light-coloured travel cases, the slimline kind. I put bright green labels on them so you'll recognise them on the carousel. Will you manage, do you think?'

Susan assured her that she would. 'I watched Vic claim his luggage when we arrived, so I know how it's done.'

'Good, then all you'll have to do is to find Uncle Ben and say your piece.' Della looked suddenly anxious, her brown eyes cloudy. 'Will you manage, do you think? We've got an awful nerve, asking you to do this. Have we asked too much?'

'I'll manage.' Susan made her voice confident, her smile reassuring. 'I'm looking forward to a glimpse of a Caribbean island—even if I'm sent packing tomorrow!'

They had both kissed her when they saw her off and stood waving and holding hands until she passed out of sight. Their blissful happiness at being together made it all worthwhile, Susan told herself. She *must* somehow manage to convince Della's godfather of the truth of the situation, so there might be a happy ending.

The crowd in the arrivals lounge was thinning a little now, and still he hadn't appeared. The butterflies in Susan's tummy began to flutter more urgently. What if the arrangements had gone wrong somehow? She couldn't have missed him here; the airport lounge was tiny in comparison with the enormous chaotic turmoil of Heathrow, through which Vic had led her so expertly.

She fidgeted with the clasp of her handbag, wondering if she should find a telephone and look up the number of Benjamin Caldicott—it must be in the book. She would give him another five minutes and then do that.

People were beginning to gather again now, no doubt to meet the next flight due in. It was a relaxed, happy atmosphere, everyone in bright-coloured, casual clothes, and everyone with a delicious sun-tan. Susan felt conscious of her pale skin, product of a London winter. She was wearing a straw-coloured skirt and top (hastily purchased yesterday, to travel in) and she realised now that particular shade simply cried out for a lovely sun-tan to match it. She only hoped she would be staying here long enough to acquire it.

She scanned the lounge again, definitely worried now. Two small boys in jazzy shorts had evaded their parents and were climbing over the seat she was sitting on. She watched them for a few moments, amused at their bubbling energy, and then she saw a tall man approaching purposefully from the far side of the lounge. Their father, probably, and there was a grim expression on his face that promised no good to the boys, Susan thought, waiting for the heavy hand of displeasure to fall.

But the tall man ignored the children and stopped before her. He gave her a quick, raking glance out of cold grey eyes and said, 'Miss Benton? I'm Gideon North. Sorry if you've been kept waiting. You'll be expecting Mr Caldicott, but unfortunately he wasn't able to meet you—I'll explain later about that. This your luggage?' He picked up the two cases. 'I've got my car outside. Shall we get out of the crush?'

He turned away without waiting for any response from her. Well, thought Susan, what a greeting! Her first impulse was to stay where she was, but he had her cases so she had to follow him.

He had mistaken her for Della, that was quite obvious. Probably he had seen a photograph of Della, or Uncle Ben had described her. They were so much alike that the mistake would be inevitable.

All right, Mr Gideon North, so if you don't wait for a reply you won't get one. She certainly wouldn't enlighten him. Her explanations would be made to Della's godfather and to nobody else, and in any case she had taken an immediate dislike to this man's overbearing manner and would say as little as possible to him. If this was the man that Della's father planned for Della to marry, then it was doubly fortunate that she wasn't here. A gentle, sensitive girl like Della deserved something better than another male chauvinist for a husband, as well as the one she had for a father.

She watched his back as he strode across the lounge, weaving his way unceremoniously between the knots of people standing around, not even glancing over his shoulder to see if she was following him, and she had to admit that he was an impressive figure. He moved like an athlete in his lightweight brown slacks and white shirt; you could almost see the muscles moving beneath, rippling obediently to their every command. You could imagine those powerful arms wielding a tennis racquet or a golf club with expertise. Or cutting through the water. She wondered idly if he was a super swimmer, and then pulled herself up sharply. What matter? She wouldn't want to swim with *him*.

But once out of the airport building she forgot all about Gideon North in the sudden jubilant realisation of where she was. She was actually here—on a Caribbean island—and it seemed like a kind of miracle. If it hadn't been for Della she would still have been in London—a London wet and cold and gloomy as she had left it this morning—tramping round looking for a job.

Even if she only had a single day here, even if Uncle Ben sent her back on the next flight, she owed Della a debt of gratitude and she made a silent vow to do her very best to pay that debt.

She had put her watch back before they reached Miami, and she saw now that it was still only early afternoon. She stood quite still, entranced, breathing the warm, scented air. The sky was a clear deep blue and the sunshine poured down, glinting on the cars in the car-park and the brown skins and colourful clothes of the people milling around. Everyone seemed to be in happy holiday mood, calling and laughing, and Susan had an irrational feeling of pure joy, as if something wonderful was just about to happen.

'Over here!' Gideon North's peremptory voice wakened her from her day-dream and she saw that he was standing beside a white, open sports car, a very impressive number indeed. She had seen cars like that gleaming behind the plate-glass of London showrooms, the prices soaring into five figures.

She almost giggled. Meeting Gideon North was certainly not the wonderful thing she had had in mind.

She wasn't going to run to obey his command. She sauntered across and settled herself in the passenger seat as he stood with barely concealed impatience, holding the door open for her. Once she was inside he slammed the door shut and climbed in behind the wheel. The car roared into life and he backed it skilfully round and out into the road.

He glanced at her and said, 'Afraid I'm rushing you—sorry about that.' He didn't sound sorry, he sounded offhand and unfriendly. 'The fact is that this couldn't have come at a worse time. I'm in the middle of a very ticklish business deal involving a hell of a lot of other people's money and I shouldn't actually be away from my office now.'

Susan said stiffly, 'You needn't have met me. If Uncle Ben couldn't come to the airport, then I could have found my own way——'

'You don't know the circumstances yet,' he rapped out. He put his foot down on the accelerator and the powerful car leapt forward to overtake a slower one, laden with young holidaymakers, who waved and whistled as they passed. 'Ben couldn't come because he isn't here. He was taken ill early this morning. There's a hospital here, but they couldn't cope with Ben's particular ailment; they flew him to the U.S. a couple of hours ago. They seemed to think an operation would be necessary.'

'Oh,' said Susan blankly. 'Oh dear, that's bad.' She bit her lip, her mind racing to try to adjust to this new set of circumstances. What on earth should she do now?

But she didn't have to make any decisions—Gideon North was making them for her. 'I'm taking you straight back to the condo apartment Ben and I share,' he said. 'That seems the obvious thing to do. I'll have to leave you there and get back to my office. We can make arrangements for your return later.'

After that he didn't seem inclined to talk and certainly Susan had no wish to. All her pleasure in being here had evaporated into a troubled confusion. She was vaguely aware that the car was passing through a small town with a shopping centre, and, further on, what looked like a business quarter with large modern buildings. Soon they were out on a dusty, sun-baked road, bordered by trees and wide-leaved shrubs which passed in a blur. Here and there, to her left, she caught a glimpse of luxurious new buildings, shining whitely beyond lawns and banks of flowering trees. The man beside her drove swiftly, but even then Susan got the impression that he was holding the powerful car in check—and holding himself in check at the same time. She looked at his hands on the wheel, the fingers brown and sinewy, guiding the car with controlled tension.

Soon they swung off the road and passed along a driveway with bushes to either side, starred with bright yellow flowers, and tall palm trees waving their feathery fronds. Turning a corner brought them into a courtyard in front of a long white building with lawns and more flowers and a swimming pool edged with white tiles, the turquoise blue water glittering in the sunshine.

Gideon North leaned over and pushed open the car door on Susan's side and she stepped out, looking up at the building in wonder.

'Why—why, it's enormous!' she gasped. 'Is this Uncle Ben's house?'

He slammed the car door with an irritable glance in her direction. 'I told you—it's a condo. A condominium,' he added, leaning into the back of the car to pull out her cases. 'Come along.'

Susan felt completely bewildered. She had never heard of a condominium, but she guessed now, from the shape of the frontage and from the number of cars parked at the side of the building, that it was some kind of hotel, or motel, or apartment block. In a daze she followed Gideon North up a flight of shallow steps, under an ornamental canopy, and through a blue painted door leading into a square, cool hall with a blue carpet and white walls.

That was all she had time to notice before he dumped down her cases and said, 'There you are, that's all I can do for you at present. You'll have to look round and find what you want—drinks and so on,' he added vaguely, already on his way out of the door again. 'I'll be back later—can't say exactly when.'

He turned away abruptly and went out and moments later Susan heard the roar of a well-tuned engine die away along the road outside.

'Well!' she said again.

She left her luggage where it was and walked into a sitting room. Here the sunshine was broken by slatted blinds, and bars of shadow lay across the blue carpet. It was a modern room. The thick carpet ran in from the hall to cover the whole floor space like a deep lake. There were comfortable lounge chairs covered in dark blue linen; tables and built-in fittings in polished wood; modern pictures which looked as if they might be originals. It was rather an austere, no-nonsense room and it certainly didn't have the kind of homely clutter that one might expect one's elderly godfather to surround himself with.

But Gideon North had said, 'the condo apartment Ben and I are sharing'. What did that mean, exactly, and how would it affect her?

She couldn't think straight until she had had a long cool drink. In the tidy kitchen she found fruit juice and ice and drank down two glasses of it. The taste was unfamiliar but heavenly.

The kitchen was super. All the equipment you could imagine—sink unit, split level cooker, washer, dryer, dishwasher, fridge—a housewife's dream. Only there wasn't a housewife here, was there? Or did Gideon North's wife live here too? No, because Della had said her father had his eye on Gideon for her—Della—so he couldn't be married. And Uncle Ben was a widower.

So that meant that if Uncle Ben was away in hospital there would be nobody but Gideon North and herself sleeping here. Oh no, she thought, she couldn't take that. Not that he would fancy her; from the almost contemptuous way he had regarded her during their short encounter up to now she was pretty sure he wouldn't. But even the idea of sharing an apartment with him made her heart begin to thump nervously.

She went up to the first floor. Here were three bedrooms and two bathrooms. Two of the bedrooms seemed to be in use, having brushes and toilet preparations laid out on the dressing tables. The third bedroom showed no sign of being occupied, so this must be the one intended for her use. Like the downstairs rooms it was luxuriously equipped. A cool green leaf-pattern covered the walls and the carpet and built-in fitments were of ivory. Floor-length windows opened on to a balcony, and she stepped out, and then drew in her breath with delight.

In front of her, as far as she could see in each direction, stretched a band of shimmering white sand, dotted with palms and other low-growing trees. Here and there brown bodies reclined on loungers or sauntered along the edge of the water, or swam in the glassy smooth lagoon. Further out the sea changed colour, became a deep blue with white flecks of spume. That would be one of the famous coral reefs of the Caribbean. And where there was a coral reef there would be an underwater world of fantastic beauty.

Susan was suddenly gripped by excitement. Everything had happened so quickly that she had given no particular thought to this place, except that it would be lovely to have a few days in a tropical island.

But to be able to dive again! The prospect began to unfold before her in all its tempting fascination. In South Devon, where she and her father had lived before his ill-considered decision to move to London, Susan had spent all her summer holidays in and out of the sea. Her father was an expert diver and he had taught her, carefully and thoroughly, first with simple snorkel equipment and later—when she showed a flair for the sport—she had progressed to learning the complete technique of diving with an aqualung. At the end of her final year at school she had enrolled for a training course at a diving establishment and—rather to her surprise—turned out to be the star pupil.

She remembered now how proud her father had been of her when she had mastered all the skills and taken her certificate.

'You're a real water baby, my Sue,' he had said, and he had bought her a properly-fitted wet-suit for her seventeenth birthday.

That summer holiday had been the most wonderful of Susan's whole life. The days were long and hot and the small cove, quite near to their cottage, almost undiscovered by tourists. Her father had worked at his painting in the mornings while Susan coped with the necessary domestic chores. Then, in the afternoons, they had loaded their equipment on to the backs of their bikes and ridden down to the cove.

The magic of those underwater expeditions! The exquisite gardens of waving seaweeds, dark green and pale green and red, growing in rockeries set in yellow sand. The rainbow-coloured fish nibbling at the rocks, darting away at their approach, the spider crabs that hid in crannies. There was always something new to see. It was sheer enchantment and she wanted it never to end.

When her father had told her they were going to have to leave and go to London at the end of that summer Susan was devastated.

'But the sea—the diving——' she had faltered, her big brown eyes full of tears.

'I know, love,' Jonathan French had agreed, 'I'm going to hate leaving it too, but we'll come back—next summer maybe. I've got to take this teaching job that's on offer. Sales have dropped off lately and Joe Barnes told me last week that he's got to close the gallery in Exeter down, so there goes my chief outlet. We've got to be realistic, sweetheart——' her father, who was the least realistic man in the world! '—and I can't let you live like a—a pretty little beachcomber.'

'But—but——' she wailed, '—you've spent so much on me. All my gear, and the lessons must have cost quite a bit. And—and you couldn't afford it. Oh, you shouldn't have!' She had wept bitterly.

He had put his arms around her. 'Don't cry, sweetheart, it'll all come right, you'll see. We'll work hard in London and save up and some day we'll go diving together on some tropical island where there's a coral reef.'

Susan stood on the balcony looking down at the

scene below and everything blurred before her eyes. If only he could have been here to see his dream come true! Somehow she must make it come true—for herself alone as he couldn't be here with her. That would have made him happy she thought, with a lopsided smile, to know she was here in this magic place.

After a while she went back into the bedroom. It was hot inside the apartment but not suffocatingly hot, and a faint breeze came in through the open window. There were switches on the wall that she took to be air-conditioning, but she wasn't going to risk using them.

She went downstairs again and carried the two travel bags up to the bedroom and opened them, balancing them on two small chairs. These were Della's cases, of course, and all the contents were Della's, for Susan's use. That was what they had arranged.

She took them out of their tissue wrappings with rising pleasure. They were beautiful—colourful little cotton sun-dresses and play-suits, skirts, tops, a selection of bikinis. Everything a girl could wish for in the way of make-up—even to a little box with false eyelashes. They might be fun to experiment with.

The second case held two wispy evening dresses, a gorgeous white lace shawl, several pairs of sandals of different colours, and a heap of flimsy pants and bras.

Susan stood still for a moment, thinking hard, looking at all this tempting gear. Della was relying on her to 'hold the fort' and hold the fort she would. From now on, until Uncle Ben's return, she was going to *be* Della Benton, come what might. If snags arose she would deal with them as they came along.

'Here goes,' she said aloud. She stripped off the clammy travelling suit gratefully and padded into the adjoining bathroom, taking a selection of Della's pots and bottles with her. Here she revelled in a cool shower, patted herself all over with toilet water that smelled of rosemary and orange, and returned to the bedroom.

It felt warmer in her now. She lay down on the silky bed quilt and stretched out her legs luxuriously. It felt lovely just to lie here after all the hours of sitting—sitting in the plane, sitting at the Miami airport waiting for Della, sitting at the Grand Cayman airport waiting for Uncle Ben who didn't come, sitting in the man Gideon North's sleek sports car. She wasn't really tired, she was sure she wasn't; she felt too excited and tensed up for that. But it was nice just to stretch out without any clothes on, on this smooth soft bed.

Jet-lag crept up on her rather suddenly. One moment she was lying here thinking of nothing very much, feeling curiously empty and strange. Then her eyes closed. A few moments later she was asleep.

She wakened with a start and it was almost dark. She had been dreaming and in her dream she had been diving down into clear, green water. Down—down—down—with fear gripping at her inside as she knew she was going too deep and that something terrible was about to happen. She struggled to rise, gasping, choking, but there was a weight holding her down.

Then she was wide awake, lying naked on the bed, and there was the dark shape of a man above her, a hand on each of her shoulders.

'What is this—an invitation? You don't waste much time, do you?'

Gideon North's voice, deep and contemptuous, shot through her muddled consciousness like a flash of lightning through a thundercloud. Her eyes widened and she tried to struggle up, but he kept his hands where they were.

'Let me go—I don't—I'm not——' she managed to get out.

His face was in shadow, but she thought he smiled and she didn't like the look of that smile at all. 'Oh no, not yet,' he said smoothly. 'If a girl chooses to lie naked on a man's bed she's likely to get what's coming to her.'

The dark blur of his face came nearer and his mouth came down on hers. She was helpless to resist, pinned down by the pressure of his hands, and his mouth took what it wanted from hers, forcing her lips apart not at all gently until she felt she was suffocating from the hard, almost brutal exploration.

She kicked out feebly with her legs, but then he was beside her on the bed, one leg thrown across hers, imprisoning her where she lay. His mouth still held hers while his hands moved down from her shoulders and round her back, drawing her body against the hardness of his, and she felt the brush of silk against her flesh and knew he was wearing nothing more than a dressing gown.

She struggled against his strength, but even as she did so she was aware of a thrill of excitement that ran all through her like a warm, weakening tide. Oh no, *no*! The words formed themselves somewhere in her mind, but horrifyingly she felt herself yielding, just as she had sunk deeper and deeper into the clear green water in her dream.

She must have stopped struggling, for his mouth came up from hers and he eased himself a little away from her, freeing his arms so that his hands could move softly and caressingly over her smooth skin. Then sanity took over and Susan shot up in the bed, pushing him away from her with all her strength. Taken by surprise, he shifted his weight until she felt herself free. Then, with the strength of panic, and sobbing under her breath, she dragged the silk cover round her and half fell off the bed, stumbling towards a dark rectangle in the wall that looked like a doorway.

It was the doorway into the bathroom. She was trapped, helpless. She came painfully up against the cold hard edge of the bath, turned round, caught her foot in the bed-cover and collapsed in a heap on the floor.

Overhead, a light came on and she put a hand across her eyes, blinking against the white dazzle. Gideon North stood in the doorway, looking down at her, completely composed, the cord of his silk gown knotted round him.

'You can get up,' he said, as Susan shrank back against the side of the bath. 'Rape isn't on my mind. In the circumstances, I naturally took it that the lady was willing.'

She struggled to her feet, still grabbing the ivory silk cover round her. 'W-what circumstances?' she stammered. 'I don't know what you're talking about.'

'No?' His tone was very dry. 'Well, I suggest you put some clothes on and we have a drink together. Any explanations can follow. For the moment I'll allow you the use of my bedroom, as you seem to have taken possession of it anyway.'

He walked out of the room and closed the door behind him. Susan went over to the case on the bed and fumbled through Della's clothes for something to wear—something that covered up as much of her as possible.

Her hands were shaking as she tossed over the contents of the case. This would have to do—a crisp cotton dress, a splash of scarlet and navy against white. She held it up and looked at it. It was sleeveless with a frill round the neck and hem, but at least it was calf-length and couldn't be construed as inviting by that—the *beast* of a man. She put on pants and a bra and slipped the dress over her head. There was a row of small buttons down the front of the bodice and it was some time before her fingers steadied themselves enough to get them fastened.

She lingered over her make-up, trying to pull her scattered wits into some sort of order, trying not to dwell too much on the episode that had just taken place. But it wasn't easy. She was still sensuously conscious of the feeling inside her, compounded of fear and excitement, that had taken over when Gideon North's arms held her and his mouth claimed hers. She was over twenty. She had been kissed before. She had been propositioned more than once. But never—never for a second—had she experienced this devastating flame of awareness that had burned through her at Gideon North's touch. Never before had she felt any need or desire to match a man's rising passion with her own. Always she had known the moment to stop before things got out of hand and somebody got hurt.

But just now had been something entirely new and different, and she wondered, as she became calmer, whether she wouldn't be well advised to tell Gideon North the truth and take the next plane back to London.

But she had promised Della ...

She stared at her reflection in the mirror and saw the face that was so like the other girl's. The same dreamy brown eyes set in a small oval face; the same clear, fine skin with just a hint of colour in the cheeks; the same lint-fair hair curving naturally into her neck just as

Della's did. The only real difference (of which Susan wasn't aware) was in the chin. There was a firmness and resolution here where Della's mouth and chin had shown only sweetness and pliancy.

Susan set her mouth now. She'd been crazy to take on this mad ploy, she shouldn't have done it. But she *had* taken it on, and for the moment she had to go on acting a role, at least until Della got in touch and they could decide what to do. As for Gideon North—Della had never met him, she had said that. So the 'circumstances' he had been hinting darkly about must simply be that she had had the misfortune to fall asleep in a bedroom that had turned out to be his, and given him all the wrong ideas. That mistake could easily be cleared up and she would certainly convince him that she was issuing no invitations. Oh yes, Mr Gideon North, you would be left in no doubt about that!

Susan lifted her small fair head high and marched down the stairs and into the sitting room. Gideon North was wearing lightweight brown trousers and a cream silk shirt, and was sitting stretched out in a lounge chair, a drink on the glass-topped table beside him. He got up as soon as she came in and went across the room to a built-in bar which he must have pulled out from the sliding door in the wall, and which glittered with bottles and glasses.

'What's your tipple?' he asked casually. She might have just dropped in for a chat instead of—instead of——

She thrust the memory away. She must not—she *would* not think about it. If she kept on remembering, it was going to be impossible to talk to this man, and she had to talk to him, to find out exactly how things stood.

'Something long and cool, please,' she said stiffly. 'I

leave it to you.' She took a chair on the opposite side of the low table, as far away from his as possible.

He mixed a drink and set it on the table beside her in its tall glass, swishing it round until the ice clinked. 'My own concoction,' he said. 'See how you like it.'

He sat down again and as she sipped her drink she was aware of his eyes fixed intently on her and it brought back the shaking feeling inside. He said, 'You're prettier than your photograph.'

She glanced round the room. 'There's no photograph of me here. Where did you see it?'

'In the drawing room of your home in London. A real eye-catcher it was, in a silver frame. It caught *my* eye.' He gave her a significant sort of smile that made her toes curl up inside their white sandals.

'Oh,' she said, playing for time. 'I—I didn't know you'd been there—I must have been out.'

He nodded. 'You were,' he said. 'I enquired. A pity I couldn't wait to meet you, but I had a plane to catch. I was on my way back here, and I merely dropped in at Ben's request with some papers for your father. We agreed, your father and I, that you were a very attractive lady.'

He was watching her closely, just as if he knew they shared some secret and was waiting for her to admit the fact.

But Della Benton shared no secret with this man. She didn't even know him—she had said so.

Susan looked at him and quickly away again. 'Thank you,' she said shortly.

'I think it must have been about that time that your father arranged this visit for you.'

She sipped her drink, crossing her legs in a non-chalant fashion but taking care to flip the skirt of the cotton dress over them. 'Possibly,' she said distantly. 'I wouldn't know.'

The man put down his glass and sat back, and his grey eyes, cold as gun-metal, passed slowly, insolently, from her face down the length of her body and back again in a deliberate way that made the blood rush into her cheeks. 'Are you trying to make me believe that you don't know why your father sent you out here?'

'Of course I know. To have a holiday and visit my godfather.'

A smile that was hardly a smile at all touched the long, straight mouth. 'Is that all? Are you quite sure about that?'

Susan had had enough of his innuendoes. Della might be timid and biddable—she wasn't. 'Look, Mr North,' she said hardily, 'I haven't the faintest idea what you're talking about, except that you seem to be making some sort of inexplicable suggestion about me, or about—about J.B.' Somehow she couldn't manage to say 'my father'.

The heavy dark brows went up. 'Is that what you call him?'

'Everyone does,' she said. Or if they didn't they were going to from now on, she decided grimly.

He nodded. 'J.B. it is, then.' He was looking slightly puzzled now. 'Are you telling me the truth?' he insisted. 'Your father—J.B.—didn't mention me at all?'

This was a tricky one. She shook her head vaguely. 'I've got an idea at the back of my mind that I may have heard your name, but he often talks about his business acquaintances, so I wouldn't be sure.'

There was a long, long silence in which he never took his eyes from her face. Just as she was beginning to feel like screaming he relaxed and said, 'Okay then, we'll play it your way. It might even be more interesting.' He got up and poured himself another drink. He came back and sat down again. 'Right,' he said, briskly now. 'We'd better make some arrangements. You do intend to stay on, I suppose?'

'Of course I do,' she said, equally brisk. 'I want to see Uncle Ben as soon as he's better and can come home. This *is* his home?'

'Well—kind of. Actually, I rent it, but Ben and I have a temporary arrangement to share, until the villa he's building for himself out at Cayman Kai—that's the other end of the island—is ready for occupation. He lived in one of the big hotels previously, but he got tired of that, so we thought this a good arrangement.' He eyed her narrowly. 'As your godfather isn't here you might care to move into a hotel yourself?'

A hotel? Goodness no, that would cost the earth in a place like this. Della had given her money, but not enough to cover something like that.

'I don't think——' she began cautiously, and he broke in to say, 'If you're worried about the cash supply I could arrange that for you. I'd open an account for you with my bank here.'

'No,' she said quickly, 'I don't want to do that.' Impersonation was bad enough; forgery was definitely *out*! 'I—I don't think I'd like to stay alone in a hotel.'

There was a sudden gleam in the grey eyes that were still fixed on her. He looked disgustingly self-satisfied.

'Ah!' he said. 'You'd prefer to stay on here—with me?'

She was in a flat spin by now, improvising at every step. She shrugged. 'I should prefer to stay in Uncle Ben's home, let's put it that way. And as this is Uncle Ben's home—yes, then I prefer to stay here. I suppose there are locks on the bedroom doors,' she added, pleased at the steadiness of her voice. 'We don't want any more misunderstandings, do we?'

To her utter surprise he burst out laughing. 'You know, Della Benton, you interest me. I think we might get along quite well together.'

Her brown eyes, so deceptively docile, met his. 'I doubt that very much,' she said crisply. 'Now, will you please tell me about Uncle Ben. Where is he, and how serious is this illness, and when is he likely to be back here?'

He was still looking slightly amused, which made her bristle with annoyance, but he answered quite concisely. 'He's in a hospital in Houston, Texas. Apparently they have special facilities to deal with his complaint, which is, I understand, some rather complex failure of liver function. How serious it is I don't yet know, but I intend to phone the hospital later today. There is, of course, no answer yet to your last question. I have no idea when he'll be back.'

Susan nodded. 'I'm so sorry about this. I suppose there's nothing at all I can do?'

'Not much, I fear, at this stage.'

'There must be something. Couldn't I send a message, or flowers by telephone or—well, anything to let him know he's not forgotten? He must be feeling absolutely wretched.' She hadn't any need to put on an act now. Della had said Uncle Ben was a sweetie, and already she felt a warm spot in her heart for him, as if he were really her own godfather, who had died when she was three years old.

'Flowers—yes, that's a nice thought. You can trek into George Town tomorrow and order them yourself.' He looked at her keenly. 'You're fond of Ben, aren't you?'

'He's a sweetie,' she said warmly, echoing Della's very words.

He nodded. 'I agree. Though I might not put it exactly like that. He was worried about your turning up and finding him not here. I told him I'd meet you and see you were okay. Of course——' he slid her an enigmatic glance '—of course he didn't know the whole story. I doubt if he'd have liked the idea of leaving you in my hands if he had.'

Susan finished her drink. It was deliciously fruity with a tang of something stronger. She needed the 'something stronger' to give her a little courage. She had to challenge this man right away and find out exactly what he was being so mysterious about. There was obviously something he expected her to know—or rather, expected Della to know—and it was going to be difficult to go on acting a part until she knew what it was.

She lifted brown candid eyes to his grey sceptical ones. 'I really am rather tired of all your hints, Mr North. I can't ignore them any longer. I think you should tell me what you're talking about. What *is* this "whole story" that Ben doesn't know?'

His look narrowed. 'You put on a good act, Miss Della Benton. Very artless and innocent. Is it a special technique of your own?'

Anger was displacing fear, as it sometimes did with Susan. 'I haven't a clue what you mean,' she said hotly, 'and I resent very much the tone you're using.'

He smiled nastily. 'Don't give me that, you know damn well what I mean.' He wasn't even pretending to be polite any longer. The glittering grey eyes moved over her with insolent appraisal. 'You know damn well why your father sent you out here.'

'I've told you—to visit my godfather. Why do you keep on and on about it?

She sat up very straight in her chair. She was so

angry that it was difficult to stay sitting down, but if she marched out of the room she wouldn't know where to go.

He tossed off the remainder of his drink and put his glass down with a click. 'All right, if you insist, I'll spell it out, although I'd have thought you would prefer a bit more subtlety. I know why your father sent you out here, and it wasn't primarily to visit your godfather. It was because he knew that I was here. He intended that you and I should—er—get together. I'm sure you know what I mean.'

Her heart was thudding so hard she was afraid he would hear it. 'Oh yes,' she stalled, 'and why should he intend that?'

He sighed. 'You really are a glutton for facts, Della Benton. Your father knows that I happen to be in possession of certain information about the way he conducts his business. A man like your father relies heavily on his credit, as I expect you're aware, and a word or two from me in certain quarters would make his credit extremely shaky.'

Susan gasped. This was worse—much worse— than she had imagined. She was beginning to get the picture, and it was too horrible to contemplate.

'You mean—you mean——' the words came mechanically,' that J.B. has done something—dishonest? And that you're blackmailing him? That he had to agree to send me out to you as—as a sort of ransom?'

He looked up to the ceiling in exasperation. 'God, why do women always have to exaggerate so? Nothing as melodramatic as that. I don't deal in blackmail—or ransoms——' He lowered his eyes to hold hers. 'Any more than I deal in rape, as I told you earlier.'

The shock of the word made her feel suddenly sick. 'Then—then what?'

'First of all, your father isn't dishonest—at least I haven't found him so. Merely tricky. As for the blackmail bit—well, I happened to admire your photograph and your father got around to talking about you. No promises were asked for, or made, but I got the impression from what he said that you might arrive here quite soon and that your presence would be in the nature of a—let us say of a—sweetener. Do I make myself clear? The episode in the bedroom just now seemed to confirm that impression.' The long mouth pulled into a cynical smile. 'Do tell me if I'm mistaken.'

'Of course you're mistaken,' she said rather wildly. 'J.B. would never do a thing like that.'

But he would, an inner voice told her. It's just the beastly kind of thing he would do, to get himself out of a jam.

He was looking searchingly at her. 'Do you really want me to believe that you know absolutely nothing about all this? That your father never even suggested that you—er—make yourself agreeable to me?'

What *had* Della said? she thought helplessly. Something about her father having a man lined up for her out here. But she didn't know about this angle, she couldn't have done.

'Of course I know nothing about it,' she snapped, 'and I don't believe a word of it.'

They stared at each other in silence and his eyes searched hers as if he could read every thought in her mind. At that moment she almost believed he could.

Then the telephone buzzed on the desk near to him and he stretched out a hand for it and answered laconically, 'Yes? North here.' His brows went up and he kept his gaze on Susan as he spoke.'Yes,' he said. 'Yes, she's here. She arrived a couple of hours ago. I'm looking after her and we're getting along splendidly. No, I haven't heard any more news of Ben yet, I'll phone the hospital later. You'd like to have a word with Della yourself—I'll hand you over to her.'

He held out the receiver towards Susan. There was a satirical expression in the cold grey eyes and his mouth curled contemptuously. 'Your father,' he said.

CHAPTER THREE

SUSAN felt very cold, suddenly. She gripped the receiver as if it were a dangerous rattlesnake as she stood beside the desk. 'Hullo,' she said.

'Hullo, Della.' The sound of John Benton's voice, even from this distance, made her feel quite ill. 'You managed the journey okay, then. You've heard about your Uncle Ben's illness, of course?'

So he knew! Had he heard before he saw Della off that her godfather wouldn't be there to meet her, and had never told her?

'Yes,' she said, 'I've heard.'

'Speak up, Della, don't mumble. I can't hear you properly.'

'I said I've heard. I'm sorry.' Would he notice anything strange about her voice, about the way she spoke?

'Well, he's in the right place, in hospital.' John Benton wouldn't worry about anyone else, only himself and his own interests. 'You'll stay on, of course, until he's back home. My friend Gideon has promised me he'll look after you and see you have a good time. You're getting on okay with him?' She recognised anxiety in the thick voice.

'Oh yes,' she said lightly. She was horribly conscious of Gideon North himself, sitting only a couple of yards away, listening to all that was being said.

At the other end of the long line to England John Benton cleared his throat audibly. 'Be nice to him,

Della,' he said slowly, meaningly. 'He can be very useful to me in business. He's not a man I'd like to offend.'

She closed her eyes. It was true, then, what Gideon North had said. Poor Della, she thought, sickened at the thought of any girl being dominated by a father like hers.

'Did you hear me?' came the grating voice. 'Why can't you say something? I told you about North before you left, you must remember.'

Susan swallowed. 'I suppose so.'

'You're not still hankering after that other fellow, are you? Because you can damn well forget about him, I've told you. That's definitely out, my girl.'

Susan was silent.

'Did you hear me, Della? I said it's definitely *out*!' He was beginning to shout now. She could almost see the heavy-jowled face getting crimson, as she had seen it so often in the office recently.

'I heard you,' she said.

'Well, mind you remember.' There was a pause and then he went on more affably, 'Now, you stay where you are and have a good time. I'm off to Germany tomorrow and I'll be up to my eyes in work for the next week or so. I'll ring you when I get back. Goodbye then, Della. Be good.' A fat chuckle as he added, 'But not too good!'

'Goodbye.' Susan replaced the receiver quickly as if it was unclean. She went back to her chair and sat down stiffly. Every bit of her body felt tense.

Gideon North had lit a cigar. He sat back in his chair and surveyed her through a wispy cloud of smoke. 'Well,' he said, 'are you still going to play Miss Innocence after that?'

She glared at him, ignoring the question. 'When did

J.B. hear about Uncle Ben being ill? Did *you* let him know about it?'

He nodded. 'I phoned him at his office as soon as it happened. Around ten o'clock yesterday morning—that would be the middle of the afternoon in London.'

'So——' said Susan slowly. 'He knew that Uncle Ben wouldn't be here when I arrived, and he didn't tell me. He just let me come.'

He lifted dark brows. 'He would, wouldn't he? Ben's absence would make everything easier for you to—how did he put it?— to be nice to me.'

'Look,' said Susan, in desperation, 'Let's get this straight. Believe it or not—and I don't care either way—I knew nothing about this—this arrangement you seem to think you had with J.B.'

'Arrangement? Oh no, nothing as definite as that. I'm no wicked squire who threatens to foreclose on the mortgage unless the poor farmer hands over his beautiful daughter. None of that old hat stuff.' There was the faintest of grins playing round his long straight mouth. 'I'm perfectly capable of getting a woman if I want one, without any outside assistance from J.B. or anyone else. I was more amused than anything at his hints but I assure you it was all left very—fluid.'

'Well, that's the way it's going to stay,' snapped Susan. Her promise to Della didn't include offering herself as a temporary diversion to this hateful, arrogant individual in order to help Della's father out of an awkward situation. John Benton was a twister, as she herself knew. She had refused once to enter into his little games, and that stood for this one too. 'Please remember that in future, Mr North.'

He got lazily to his feet. 'As I said, we'll play it your way,' he drawled. 'Now, how about eating? I need food after a day's work. There's quite a reasonable restaurant here, I suggest we patronise it this evening. Later on, I can show you the more exotic spots. And don't you think you'd better call me Gideon? My friends do.'

She looked up at him, standing tall and relaxed above her, his hands thrust into the pockets of his lightweight brown pants, and thought he was the pattern of masculine arrogant self-satisfaction. The kind of man that most girls fall for without a struggle. The kind of man she distrusted and—yes—despised.

'I'm not sure,' she said distantly, 'that I want you for a friend.'

He made an impatient movement of his broad shoulders. 'Oh, don't overplay the act, for God's sake. Come along, let's eat, I'm hungry.' And he took both her hands and pulled her to her feet, holding her against him for a brief moment before he let her go. She recoiled as if she had touched a live electric wire, the blood suddenly beating through her body. The intimate gesture might have been merely a casual man-woman recognition, or it might have been the promise of something far more intimate to come.

But there was no point in fighting with him at this moment, Susan decided, as he opened the door for her to pass out. She would need all her strength and all her wits about her for later on. And the thought of what 'later on' might turn out to be made her knees shake.

Outside in the darkness the air was warm, full of the scent of lush growing things. Lights twinkled from low buildings, half hidden among the trees. Music drifted out through open windows and from quite near came the sleepy swell and splash of the sea.

Susan walked beside Gideon along a paved way between lawns and shrubs and wondered how she could find out about the set-up here. Della, presumably, would know all about a millionaires' playground like this place and the man beside her might begin to get really suspicious if she seemed too ingenuous and naïve. Still, that was something she must risk. She could never in this world keep up the pretence of being a rich man's daughter, accustomed to all the good things of life. That would be far too much of a strain, and anyway this Gideon person with his penetrating gaze would see through it in no time. So she would just be her own self and hope she could hold the fort for Della for a few days. After that it wouldn't matter about Gideon North and what he thought or believed.

She waved a hand around. 'Does all this belong to the condo?'

'This *is* the condo,' he said. 'One of the many along Seven Mile Beach. The Caymans are heart and soul in the tourist business.'

'Seven miles of beach—really?'

'Really. This particular bit of it is our own private paradise, if you care to look at it like that.' His voice was faintly ironic. 'There's a tennis court and a swimming pool. And that, my girl, is about all that Grand Cayman has to offer. No casino, no TV, no sightseeing, no trendy night-life. I'm thinking that a sophisticated young lady may be very rapidly bored here.'

She glanced up at the hard profile, thrown into stark relief by the lights from one of the apartment buildings they were passing. It wouldn't be easy, but she somehow had to hold her own with this formidable man or he would grind her into the ground.

'Meaning me?' she challenged him.

'Who else?'

'I don't see myself like that,' she said. 'And I certainly

won't be bored. There's the sea, isn't there?'

'Oh yes,' said Gideon, as if he had lost interest in the subject of her entertainment. 'There's the sea.'

They came to a low, discreetly floodlit building, in the middle of a clearing of trees. 'This is our own club-house,' said Gideon. 'Come along in and I'll introduce you to Owen Richards, the manager.'

Inside was luxury—everything spacious and modern and perfectly appointed. A slight, coffee-skinned man in a white jacket came across the foyer to greet them. 'Evening, Mr North, nice to see you. You dining with us tonight?' He spoke with a delightful soft lilt that sounded Welsh to Susan's ears.

'Hullo, Owen. Yes, we'd like to sample your fare. I've brought Mr Caldicott's niece along, she's just arrived.'

The little man bowed and grinned delightedly. 'Very pleased to meet you, Miss——'

'Benton,' said Susan, and it came out quite naturally. It was getting easier to think of herself as Della Benton now.

'Miss Benton.' He grinned and bowed again. 'We were very sorry to hear about Mr Caldicott's illness. Such a very nice gentleman. Can I enquire how he is?'

'We don't know much yet,' Gideon told him. 'I'm phoning the hospital later.'

The little man nodded gravely. 'I trust the news is good, sir. Will you have drinks sent here or go into the dining room?'

'We'll go straight in, Owen, and if you could hurry up our order I'd appreciate it. Miss Benton's been tra-velling for a long time and is tired. What can you sug-gest that you could serve up quickly?'

'Steak and salad, sir? Or lobster?'

Gideon glanced at Susan. 'Which, Della?'

'Oh, lobster, please. That sounds simply delicious.'
She smiled at the manager, hovering eagerly, and he
seemed to grow about an inch.

Gideon said, 'I'll have the same. Avocado to start?'

Owen Richards beamed at them both. 'Certainly, Mr
North. Five minutes, sir. I'll send Martine in for your
wine order.' He hurried away importantly.

Gideon slanted an ironic look at Susan. 'Nicely done!
I imagine you find that smile of yours very useful.'

Her hand itched to smack that twisted grin off his
face, but she restrained herself and said coldly, 'Do you
make a habit of suspecting everybody's motives, Mr
North?'

'Gideon,' he said easily, taking hold of her bare arm
to lead her towards a glass door at the other end of the
foyer. His fingers were warm and very firm, and in spite
of her surge of annoyance she felt her pulses flutter at
his touch.

He appeared to consider her question. 'Not everybody's. I'm just particularly wary about the motives of
beautiful young women.'

He pushed open the door and immediately a young
West Indian waiter with a flashing smile came forward
to lead them to a table outside, on a thatched patio.

As they passed through the cool, intimately-lit, low-
ceilinged room Susan had a fleeting impression of the
satiny bare shoulders of the girls above their flimsy
colourful dresses; of the well-groomed heads of the
men; of laughter and the clink of glasses and cutlery; of
the scent of flowers and well-cooked food; of leisure
and luxury and enjoyment.

At several of the tables Gideon was greeted by name
as they walked past. He returned the greetings amiably
but with no great enthusiasm, and he made no attempt

to stop and introduce her. These people, Susan supposed, would mostly be her new neighbours in the other apartments. It would be pleasant if she could find someone to be friendly with while she was here.

On the patio she sank into the chair the waiter held back for her and looked round with delight. This was paradise—straight out of the travel brochures she had pored over yearningly and hopelessly. This was everything she had ever imagined in her most romantic dreams of far-away places. Beyond the patio, lights winked among the dense foliage. The leaves of the palm trees rustled faintly above. And then, as if right on cue to complete the picture, a half-moon rose in the starstudded black velvet of the sky.

Susan clasped her hands. 'What an absolutely heavenly spot!'

Gideon surveyed her radiant face, with her brown eyes glinting in the muted glow of the table lamp, her lips parted softly, and his brows rose quizzically. 'Don't tell me a tropical island playground has anything new to offer Miss Della Benton.'

'Why not?' She had a sudden desire to argue with him. 'Things don't have to be new to be appreciated.'

He shrugged slightly, his look still holding hers. 'But there's always a special allure about anything new. Or any*one*,' he added in a lazy drawl that held a meaning she couldn't possibly miss.

He wasn't going to give up, was he? He had decided that she had come out here to entice him into an affair and he wasn't going to let either of them lose sight of that fact.

Their meal arrived and Susan applied herself hastily to the avocado, as her heartbeats quickened uncomfortably. At least she could enjoy the food, and until now avocado had been a luxury item, out of her price range. She found it delicious, and even more delicious was the lobster that followed, cradled in creamy salads and accompanied by crisp, freshly baked rolls.

'All right for you?' Gideon enquired politely.

'Lovely! I didn't know I was so hungry.'

He poured wine into her glass. 'The cooking here isn't exactly Cordon Bleu, but Owen has a good, middle-of-the-road chef whom he imported from Martinique and he puts on some excellent French meals when the spirit moves him. But George Town has a good assortment of restaurants, mostly of the ethnic variety—Chinese, Italian, Spanish, etc. And of course the big hotels put on really superb meals. I must take you to the Holiday Inn one evening, it's quite something.'

Susan looked up. 'You don't have to entertain me, you know.'

The grey eyes glittered with amusement. 'It will, as the saying goes, be my pleasure. And—I hope—to my eventual advantage.'

Before Susan could think of a come-back to this blatant statement of intent he added, 'Besides, before he left, your Uncle Ben particularly asked me to give you a good time and not let his illness spoil your holiday. So you see, we both have been instructed to amuse each other. Coincidence, isn't it?' His eyes narrowed wickedly. 'It would be a pity, don't you think, for either of us to renege on our briefs?'

'Oh!' gasped Susan. 'You're quite impossible!'

He laughed aloud and topped up her glass. 'This I'll say for you, Della Benton, you have an original line in allurement. Intended to intrigue, I take it?'

She took a sip of wine and put down her glass deliberately. 'I've no intentions of any sort where you're concerned, Mr North, and you can believe that or not, as you like.'

He lounged back in his chair. 'Frankly, I don't believe it. But, as I said, we'll play it your way. The game has a certain astringent quality that might be amusing. I never cared for ripe fruit that melts in the mouth.'

She flared with resentment. Everything she said was twisted round to fit in with his own horrid suspicions. 'All right!' She flung the words at him under her breath. 'If you're determined to think the worst about me and my motives, I can't stop you.'

The ironic smile again. 'Too true you can't. And anyway, when I've made up my mind about something I don't relish argument. Now, what would you like to follow the lobster? They do a very good coconut ice-cream.'

'Thank you,' she said stiffly. She needed something to cool the hot anger seething inside her.

But it was no good letting herself get too worked up about this disgustingly arrogant individual. At the moment he was the only person she knew on the island, and her one source of information.

So she asked him questions and learned that the beach and the sea were the main attractions of the Caymans—really the only attractions.

'You can sunbathe to your heart's content, of course,' he told her, adding, with a glance at her delicate pale skin, 'only for goodness' sake take it slowly at first and cover up. The sun's very potent here and you don't know you're getting burned until it's too late. I've seen it happen more than once.'

End of lecture, she thought, gritting her teeth. But she merely said, 'I'll remember. But what I really want is to get into the sea. There's a coral reef here, isn't there'

He looked curiously at her. 'You don't know your Caribbean very well, do you?'

Her inside gave a small jolt. Did he suspect she wasn't the girl she seemed to be—the rich man's daughter who would be familiar with the world's luxury playgrounds? If he really challenged her she wasn't sure that she could keep up the deception—which she hated anyway. But if she didn't, if it all came out, she would be letting Della and Vic down. She was sure that Gideon North wouldn't have the understanding and compassion to help.

'I don't know the Caribbean at all,' she said shortly. 'But most people have heard about the coral reefs around the islands.'

He seemed to have lost interest in the conversation. There was obviously someone he knew in the dining room and he was acknowledging a greeting with a smile. Susan watched the hard face soften when he smiled and wondered what it would be like if he smiled at her—really smiled, as he was doing now. Not the amused, critical, enigmatic smile he had so far treated her to, but the real thing. It made him look quite different—and, she had to admit, rather devastatingly attractive.

He turned his attention back to her. 'You were asking about the coral reefs here. They're particularly fine around the Caymans—in fact they're what many visitors come for. If you want to take a look at our famous underwater world there are glass-bottomed boats that go out quite regularly.'

She ignored his faintly patronising tone. 'I wasn't thinking of glass-bottomed boats. I was thinking of diving. I suppose one can hire equipment here?'

'Oh yes, there are any number of dive shops.' He was looking at her with a little more interest now. 'Are you experienced?'

She would have rather liked to take out the B.S.A.C.

qualification record she had brought with her, along with her passport, and wave it in his face, but that would have been ridiculously childish. So she merely said, 'I did some diving when we lived in Devon, some time ago.'

'H'm.' He was regarding her speculatively, as if wondering if she could be any good. 'Well, I have a friend who runs a diving school. If you like I'll take you to see him. He's top class.'

'Thank you, I'd like that,' she said.

'But you mustn't ever go diving alone, you know, not even snorkelling. You understand that?'

'Of course,' said Susan coldly. What did he think she was—some silly nitwit who would put herself at risk and be a nuisance to other people? Yes, that was probably just what he thought. She had a very strong impression that he was one of those men who label girls 'for amusement only'.

But it didn't matter what he thought. What mattered was that he could put her in touch with someone who would arrange some diving for her, and that prospect was vastly more important than Mr Gideon North's male chauvinist opinions.

They finished dinner and left the club-house, strolling back along the shrub-bordered walk the way they had come. The moon had risen higher and the scene was bathed in light that silvered the wide, waxy leaves of the shrubs. It was very quiet and still and the air was full of aromatic scents and the only sound was the faint chirrup of insects.

Once again Susan was caught up in the sheer magic of the place and the unreality of being here, strolling through the scented moonlit evening with this stranger beside her—this handsome, maddening, arrogant man whom she could dislike and resent, but never ignore.

Almost as if he could guess her thoughts he moved closer and linked his arm casually with hers, and the touch of his fingers on her bare skin made her pulses leap. Wryly she thought that it wasn't only the sun that was very potent around these parts. You could easily get burned in other ways and wouldn't realise it until it was too late. She must be very, very careful.

They rounded a corner and came in sight of the apartment they had started from. Susan recognised it by the blue front door shining silver in the moonlight and by the bush beside it starred with yellow flowers. 'What now?' murmured Gideon, close to her ear. 'Do you want to go in or shall we——'

He stopped abruptly as two figures—a man and a woman—appeared from the direction of the adjoining apartment.

'Gideon—darling!' The girl's voice was warm and husky. 'We're back, you see. Surprised?'

Gideon didn't disengage his arm from Susan's. 'Somewhat,' he said, deadpan. 'What happened?'

'Sale fell through,' said the young man, who seemed to be wrapped in a towelling bathrobe. The moonlight fell on curly, sandy-brown hair and a pair of thin legs showed beneath the robe. 'So we thought we might as well come back for a while, until we find another buyer. How's life, Gideon?' Susan felt his gaze turn upon her expectantly.

The girl was looking at her too. Her face was in shadow, and she, too, seemed to be wearing a loose wrap of some kind. All that was clearly visible was her hair—in the moonlight her hair was jet black, a carefully-arranged tangle of coils and tendrils. Luxuriant. Striking.

'Life's been a trifle complicated,' Gideon was saying. 'Ben was taken ill yesterday and he's in hospital in the

States. This is Della Benton, his niece, who was on her way out here for a holiday when it all happened. Della, meet Faye Lord and her brother Sebastian—our next-door neighbours.'

'Oh, poor darling Ben, what a shame!' cried Faye, and her brother muttered something that sounded like 'rotten bad luck.'

'And poor you!' Faye turned to Della gushingly. 'Coming to this end-of-the-world spot all for nothing! How boring for you!'

'I'm sure I shan't be bored,' Susan said quietly. She didn't think she was going to like Faye Lord at all. 'This is my first time here and I'm sure I'm going to love it. The apartment is quite delightful,' she added.

There was a short silence. Then Faye said, 'You're staying at Gideon's apartment?' The sympathy had left her voice abruptly.

'At my Uncle Ben's apartment—yes.'

'Is there any reason why Della shouldn't be staying at the apartment, Faye?' Gideon's voice cut in on a drawling note.

'Darling, of course not.' Faye's hand fluttered from under her gown and touched Gideon's arm. 'I only thought——'

'What did you think?' he asked smoothly.

'Oh—only that she might be more comfortable at one of the hotels, as dear old Ben isn't here to look after her.'

Gideon drew Susan a little closer. 'I'm sure I'll be able to look after Della's comfort quite adequately, and she's chosen to share the apartment with me for the time being, haven't you, Della?'

Words would have choked Susan and she stood there in silence. I could kill him, she thought. If he'd said,

'She's chosen to share my bedroom with me', he couldn't have put it more plainly.

Faye made a jerky movement and the moonlight fell on her face, for a moment contorted with anger. Then she laughed, and the sound wasn't husky and warm; it was high and metallic. 'It's a good thing Ben isn't here. He wouldn't approve of such goings on.'

'Goings on?' said Gideon innocently. 'Whatever are you talking about, Faye? You should know me better than that.'

'Yes, darling,' said the girl with saccharine sweetness. 'I should, shouldn't I?'

Beside her Sebastian moved impatiently. 'Oh, come on, Sis, when you two have quite finished sparring, what about our swim? We're going down the beach, Gideon, want to come? Della?' He turned his head hopefully in Susan's direction.

'No, thanks, Seb. Not tonight. Della's tired, she's been travelling since early this morning.' Gideon answered for both of them, drawing her towards the blue front door as he spoke. 'Enjoy yourselves, you two. Be seeing you.'

It was very warm in the sitting room. Gideon switched on the light and lowered the slatted blind over the closed window. Then he flicked another switch and a large electric fan in the ceiling started to whirr.

'I prefer a fan to the air-conditioning,' he remarked conversationally. 'We have to keep the windows closed in the evening to keep out the bugs. We have our own brand here called, picturesquely, no-see-ums. You'd be well advised to lay in a stock of insect-repellant if you haven't brought any—you never know when they might strike.'

Susan stood tensely in the doorway. She was still

seething with anger at what had just happened and no amount of casual chit-chat was going to divert her.

Gideon strolled across the room and poured himself a drink. 'Nightcap?' he enquired over his shoulder.

'No, thank you,' said Susan frostily.

He turned, frowning. 'What's the matter?'

'You know very well what's the matter.'

He came towards her, glass in hand. 'No, cross my heart, I don't.'

She drew in a tight breath. 'What you did just now was quite unforgiveable!'

He shook his head, mystified. 'I'm not following you. You'll have to spell it out for me.'

Beast, she thought, he was deliberately needling her. 'Don't pretend you don't know what I mean,' she threw at him. 'You let those people think we were—were——' Humiliatingly she choked on the words.

He smiled lazily. 'Sleeping together?'

She felt the colour flood into her face and she marched past him into the room and stood with her back to the desk. 'Yes, if you put it so crudely, that's what I mean.'

'How would *you* put it?' he enquired mildly.

'It isn't a subject I'm in the habit of discussing with complete strangers,' she said distantly. She was dismally aware that she was making a complete fool of herself with this man. In the circle he moved in no doubt the subject was discussed constantly and in much cruder terms.

He was eyeing her curiously. 'What the hell does it matter what Faye and Sebastian think is going on?'

She turned her head away quickly, biting her lip to stop it trembling. Suddenly she felt very much alone in an alien world and completely out of her depth with this man who belonged so confidently in that world.

'Oh, you wouldn't understand,' she said, her eyes misting with tears of fatigue and confusion.

He looked at her in silence for a moment longer. Then he went back across the room. 'I'll mix you a drink,' he said. 'You're tired—it'll help you to sleep.'

It was the first time he had spoken to her with consideration, and her inside seemed to turn over. She sat down and took the glass he handed to her.

She sipped the liquid and felt the tingle as it trickled down her throat, stiffening her courage to say what she must say. Gideon had dropped into the chair opposite and she met his eyes resolutely. 'Look, we can't go on like this, you know. You've jumped to the wrong conclusions ever since I arrived.'

'Have I?' he queried laconically. 'How?'

He wasn't going to help her, but she soldiered on. 'Well, you've made it quite clear that—for various reasons—you expected me to be—available.'

His grey eyes glinted. 'I thought you seemed to be making that fairly clear yourself.'

'I told you,' she burst out angrily, 'that was a misunderstanding. You shouldn't have taken advantage of it.'

His mouth twitched. 'My dear girl! If you could have seen how tempting you looked spread out on my bed with a——'

'Please!' she broke in, her cheeks crimson.

'Okay, we'll leave it for now. But—as you've brought the matter up—what exactly are you trying to tell me?'

'What I'm trying to tell you is that—whatever you may think and whatever you heard J.B. say on the phone—I *did* come here to see Uncle Ben, and I *didn't* agree to act as a—a "sweetener" so that you'd overlook J.B.'s tricky ways. J.B. mentioned your name, but I didn't take much notice. I—I thought it was just to take my mind off—other things.'

That, she thought, was fairly near the truth of the matter. She was sure that Della wouldn't have concealed anything from her.

Gideon was leaning back in his chair, holding his glass in both hands and regarding her steadily over the rim. 'Ah,' he said, 'it's this other fellow, is it? The one that J.B. was talking about on the phone—the one he doesn't approve of?'

She shrugged. 'If you heard all that, then you know, don't you?'

'Are you in love with him?'

He put down his glass and leaned towards her, covering her hand with his. At his touch her heart gave a crazy lurch and she felt suddenly weak as the blood rushed through her body, burning into her cheeks. His face was so close that she could see the tiny wrinkles beside his eyes, the way his thick coppery hair grew back at the temples. She could smell the faint, astringent scent of some toilet preparation; could sense the warmth of his skin.

She stared into the steel-grey eyes so near her own and wanted quite desperately to move nearer, to feel his mouth close over hers and his arms hold her as they had held her before. It was dangerous madness.

'*Are* you, Della?' he asked again.

'Yes,' she said, pulling her hand from his.

He nodded, smiling faintly. 'We know where we are, then. But this other fellow isn't here, is he, and until he turns up I have every intention of handling the situation in my own way. And don't say I didn't warn you.' He spoke briskly, as if he had just concluded a satisfactory business arrangement.

Susan couldn't let him get away with the final word. 'I don't know what you mean by that, but please remember that I'm not in the market for a casual affair.'

'No?' he smiled. 'We shall see.'

He picked up their glasses and carried them into the kitchen, calling back to her, 'We have a maid service here, so I leave all the washing-up for her in the morning. Adèle's very willing, but she sometimes has rather hazy ideas about where things go.' He appeared in the doorway again. 'That's probably why you made the mistake about the bedrooms earlier on. She'd probably been cleaning up there and had got things mixed up. Come along up and we'll sort it out.'

Susan followed him upstairs and into the room she had been in before. Her cases still lay open on the chairs where she had put them. The dressing table was covered with Della's toilet things—brushes, combs, pots, bottles, powder. The big bed with its silky cover still showed the indentations of her body and the signs of a scuffle, although Susan had smoothed it down and replaced the cover after that traumatic encounter with Gideon earlier on. She was disturbingly aware of him now, standing just behind her, and it was an effort to steady her hands as she closed the lids of the cases and snapped the locks.

'If you'll take these in to the room I'm to have, I'll bring all the bits and pieces,' she said, and was pleased that she managed to sound practical and unflustered. 'And is it time to ring the hospital yet? I'd like to know how Uncle Ben is getting along before I go to bed.'

Gideon dumped her cases in the adjoining room and glanced at his watch. 'They told me not to ring before half-past nine. The specialist who's going to be in charge of the case is travelling down from Fort Worth. He's a top man, they say, and Ben should be in good hands. It's only just after half-nine, but I'll have a try.'

He sat down on the bed and pulled the telephone

towards him. Susan stood beside him, but not too near, and waited while the call went through. Very soon Gideon was talking to someone at the hospital. She listened to his side of the conversation—mostly, 'Yes', and 'Yes, I see', and 'I understand that', but the feminine voice at the other end was just a clacking sound.

Finally he put down the receiver and shrugged towards her. 'Not much they could tell me yet—just that he's comfortable. The Great Man hasn't arrived and probably there won't be a detailed investigation until tomorrow. We'll just have to wait.'

Susan nodded and said softly, 'It's a shame he's there all by himself.' She was thinking of how it had been when they took Daddy to hospital after the accident. He had been conscious, he had lived for two days and she had been with him almost all the time.

Her eyes were misty and she didn't see the thoughtful look on Gideon's face. He said, 'Yes—well, they seem to be looking after him very adequately. All you can do just now is to go along into George Town tomorrow and arrange for flowers and a message to be sent to him.'

She said, 'Yes, I'll do that—how do I get there?'

'There's a good taxi service—you'll find the number on the pad downstairs. Or would you like me to arrange the hire of a car for you while you're here?'

'Oh no, I'd rather use a taxi,' she said hastily. It would raise too many suspicions if she admitted that she had never learned to drive. Daddy's income had never risen to car-owning level and in Devon Susan's main mode of transport had been an ancient bike.

'Just as you like,' he said. 'I'll be backwards and forwards quite frequently. I've got some leave due to me. So I can often ferry you where you want to go.' He still sounded offhand and businesslike; it was difficult to believe that only a couple of hours ago he had held her in his arms and——

She swallowed and said, 'And will you give me the address of the hospital, please?'

He pulled the notepad on the bedside table towards him and scribbled on it.

'Thank you,' said Susan. Then, smothering a not-quite-genuine yawn, 'I really am awfully tired—I'll get to bed before I go to sleep on my feet. Perhaps you'd transfer your things to your own room?' She didn't want him knocking on her door to claim his razor or pyjamas. She glanced at him, sitting on the side of the bed, long legs stretched out before him, and wondered if he wore pyjamas, and the thought sent the blood rushing into her cheeks.

She turned quickly to the dressing table and began to put together his brushes and toilet articles and he stood up and came over the room towards her. 'Adèle must have had a brainstorm, putting my stuff in here.' He pulled open the drawers of the dressing table. 'You see? Empty. This was the room intended for you.'

'Yes, I see now,' said Susan. He was smiling his twisted smile and she was overcome by a horrid confusion. 'I—I'm sorry I made such a silly mistake.'

The grey eyes glinted beneath their ridiculously long lashes. '*I'm* not sorry,' he said.

Their eyes met and locked and she found herself quite unable to look away. Then his gaze slowly moved down and fastened itself on her mouth, and the breath seemed to leave her body. Time stood still and there was no sound, not even the ticking of a clock. Only the two of them facing each other here with a message that needed no words passing between them.

Then Gideon moved and swept up his brushes and bottles in one hand. 'Goodnight, Della,' he said softly, and, 'It's a pity about that other fellow, but I'm sure we can get over that small difficulty.'

He walked to the door. 'Look—there's a lock on your side. You'd better turn it. I'm only a man and you're a very lovely lady.'

She saw him toss his brushes on to the bed in the next room, then he crossed the landing and ran down the stairs without a backward look.

Susan closed the door and turned the key slowly. She wished there were a key on her heart.

CHAPTER FOUR

Susan opened her eyes next morning to the sound of a vacuum cleaner whirring away somewhere downstairs. She lay blinking at the ceiling above her head, trying to gather her thoughts together.

But yesterday had been quite a day. Far too much had happened to remember it all, and anyway only one thing seemed to stand out, one huge, inescapable fact, dwarfing everything else. She had met Gideon North—resented him, despised him, hated him. And ended up by falling in love with him.

Susan had never thought of herself as a girl who did things on impulse. And yet the last few days seemed to have been full of snap decisions. From the moment she defied John Benton in his office, things had crowded up on her thick and fast, forcing her to say yes or no before she had time to consider. She had been making up her mind without weighing anything up; guided by emotion alone.

She sat up in bed, tossing her silky fair hair back from her face. It had got to stop—especially this crazy notion that she had fallen in love. It had been understandable enough, she allowed herself. Yesterday had been a long, exhausting day—a day nearly twenty-four hours long, if you counted the six hours added on for crossing the Atlantic, and she had only had that one short sleep that had ended so traumatically. By the end of the day her judgments must have been well and truly incapable of working. In love with Gideon North? How utterly ridiculous! Next time she set eyes on the man she would realise her mistake. Oh, he was an attractive male, of course, alive with the kind of masculine magnetism that drew women like moths to a light. But she wasn't a moth and she recognised the danger. She hadn't come here to look for a sultry holiday romance, she had come to help Della and Vic. That was the most important thing of all. But—she had to admit—nearly as important was the prospect of getting a glimpse of a paradise island that she would never in her life be in a position to visit otherwise. She was determined to enjoy every last minute of it.

She slid eagerly out of bed and padded across the soft carpet to the window. Fabulous! To be able to look down from your bedroom window on to white powdery sand and palm trees and that green stretch of lagoon like glass under the deep blue sky!

She had slept late and her watch told her that it was after ten. She wasn't going to waste time showering and dressing; she was going to get into that sea at the first possible moment. Hastily she rummaged in Della's case and pulled out a red and white spotted bikini. She would unpack and tidy everything later, she promised herself; just now she was powered by a compelling urge to swim out there in the lagoon. The bikini fitted perfectly. She slipped on sandals, thrust a brush through her hair, threw on a red cotton cover-up, and ran downstairs. She hardly thought about Gideon, except to guess that by now he would have left for his office.

In the kitchen she found a pretty, brown-skinned girl with curly black hair and a wide, friendly smile. 'Good morning, miss. Shall I get you breakfast? Mr North said not to wake you up, you were very tired.'

Susan smiled back at her. 'I'd love some coffee, if you've got some made. You're Adèle, aren't you?'

'This is right. My father is chef in the restaurant—we come here from Martinique two years ago. The work is very good here—plenty of rich people, you know? I work here two hours each morning and two hours at the next apartment. It has been closed, but now Miss Lord and her brother have come back and I must go there again.' She wrinkled her nose expressively. 'You have milk in your coffee, yes?'

Susan drank her coffee standing up while Adèle polished glasses and stacked them on a tray, talking all the time. 'I am sorry Miss Lord has come back, she is not very nice to work for. She expects a lot. It is so much better here. Mr Caldicott, he is a lovely gentleman and so kind. And Mr North——' She rolled sloe-dark eyes. 'He is what you call a smasher!' She gave Susan a woman-to-woman grin. 'You have a good time here, yes, while old Mr Caldicott is away in hospital?'

What did you say to that? 'Mr North and I are just good friends'? Adèle wouldn't believe a word of it—and anyway it wasn't true. Gideon North wasn't the kind of man a girl can look on as a good friend. For just one moment she wondered what it would be like if she were really having an affair with him—if she were that kind of girl, *his* kind of girl. She felt suddenly breathless and pushed away the thought in alarm, tossed down the remainder of her coffee, and, with a word of explanation to Adèle, ran out of the apartment, across the lawn and down on to the beach.

There were very few signs of life about—one or two people drifting out towards the sun-beds under straw umbrellas; two men pushing out a dinghy towards a white yacht that was moored further out to sea; that was all. The fine white sand was warm under Susan's feet as she pulled off her sandals. She tossed off the red cover-up and, with a thrill of anticipation, waded out into the water.

It was all she had anticipated—and more. She dived beneath the surface and came up again, blinking, her hair streaming round her face, laughing aloud. It was exhilarating, like swimming in a sea of pale green champagne. For a moment she floated on her back, revelling in the taste of salt on her lips and the sun burning redly through her closed eyelids, then twisted like a fish and struck out for the darker line ahead that marked the reef.

It was more than three years since she had swum or dived, but by the time she reached the reef all her confidence had come back. She dived down like an arrow, but without a face-mask the underwater world was just a blur of colours and vague shapes. Also, it was difficult to manoeuvre without fins. She surfaced and let out her breath. Here she was, swimming over a coral reef and she couldn't even see it properly. It was exasperating. She must, she decided, acquire at least some snorkel equipment at the very first opportunity, and she certainly wasn't going to wait until Gideon found the time to introduce her to his friend who ran the diving school. Heavens, she thought, she might well be on her way home again by the time he got around to *that*!

She would go back to the apartment, have some breakfast, and then make her way into George Town, where she could arrange about the flowers for Uncle Ben, and about hiring some gear at the same time.

As she waded ashore she saw a man standing at the edge of the sea, watching her. Not Gideon; this man was fair and slight, not dark and tough.

'Hi, Della. Early bird, aren't you?' a laughing voice greeted her. Sebastian Lord, of course, lanky in shorts and tee-shirt.

'Hullo!' She pushed her wet hair out of her eyes, quite unaware of the picture she made, standing there in her minuscule scarlet bikini, her brown eyes sparkling with the exhilaration of her swim. Quite unaware, too, of the quick admiration in the young man's eyes. 'Not early enough. I've only had time for a short swim. It's gorgeous in the water, I could have stayed in all day.'

She bent down for her red cover-up, but Sebastian grabbed it first and draped it carefully round her. 'Do you *have* to come out? Couldn't we swim together? I could do with something to wake me up—Faye dragged me off to a barbecue last night and we were up until all hours. She's still sleeping it off.'

'Sorry.' Susan started to walk back up the beach, swinging her sandals in her hand. 'I'd have loved to, but I need to get into George Town. I want to send some flowers to Mr Caldicott—to Uncle Ben, in hospital.'

Sebastian kept beside her. 'I was thinking of going into George Town myself, as a matter of fact. I need a new D-string.'

'A new *what*?' She was a pace or two in front of him, the grass of the lawn springy and warm under her bare feet.

'A D-string. For my guitar,' he explained. 'Do let me take you.'

They had reached the apartment now and she stopped. 'Well, it's very kind of you. I was going to ring for a taxi.'

'Oh, *please* don't do that, it would break my heart.' He pulled a comical face. He had a wide, full mouth and a lot of freckles.

Susan laughed. It was pleasant to talk to an ordinary, friendly young man after Gideon North. 'I shouldn't like to do that. Thanks very much then—in about twenty minutes?'

'Fine.' He grinned in delight. 'I'll be waiting.'

Adèle had gone, leaving a breakfast tray of rolls and butter and fruit. Susan ate standing up and then dashed upstairs to shower quickly and slip on a jump-suit of coffee-coloured polycotton. It was delightfully cool and the long sleeves and ankle pants would protect her from too much sun too soon. She didn't want that bossy Gideon North saying 'I told you so' if she got badly sunburned. She slipped her feet into white sandals, picked up a white handbag and went out.

Sebastian was waiting for her on the patio and his eyes lit up when he saw her. 'Wow!' he murmured expressively.

He had changed too, into jeans and a pink shirt with wide blue stripes, which gave him a slightly clownish appearance. He led the way to a cherry-red convertible, parked in the drive, and settled her in with great care.

'This is super,' he beamed, as they joined the road. 'You being next door, I mean. I must admit I was pretty cheesed off when my papa decided that Faye and I should come back and be in residence, but now you've come things have taken a decided turn for the better. Whoopee!' He let out a wild screech as he overtook a white Mini, cutting in rather dangerously close to an oncoming bus as he did so.

Susan clutched the edge of her seat. 'Don't get too carried away,' she gasped. 'I'd prefer to get to George Town in one piece!'

'Sorry, sweetheart.' He patted her knee, pulling

nearer to the side of the road. 'Now, tell me the story of your life.'

That was the very last thing Susan had any intention of doing. 'No, you tell me yours instead.'

Sebastian sighed. 'Very boring, but if you insist—— Born Richmond, England, twenty-one years ago. Papa manufacturer of office furniture. Usual schools. Papa moves to States for period, buys condo apartment Cayman Islands for vacation amusement. Papa moves back to England, apartment for sale. Buyer makes offer. Buyer cries off. Sister Faye wheedles Papa to come back here. Sebastian persuaded somewhat against will to accompany sister. Papa won't trust her here alone, although sister of an age to look after herself. Seven years older than Sebastian, in point of fact. That's it, up to date.'

'Very pithy,' Susan smiled. 'And what are you doing now?'

'Doing?' He looked blank.

'What sort of work? University, or training for something, or what?'

'Oh—work! Well now, that's something I haven't given much thought to. My papa thinks I might go into the furniture business.' He grimaced. 'Can you see me fitting a nifty table leg?'

'Why not? Somebody has to, if we're to have tables.'

He pulled his clown's face. 'I can see you're a practical girl. Well, if you're really interested—which nobody else is—I rather fancy myself as a composer of popular songs.' He laughed—rather selfconsciously, she thought. 'You should hear my last one. Very touching little ballad.'

Susan glanced at his face. He looked very young. 'I'd like to hear it,' she said.

'You would?' He gave a whoop. 'Hurrah! Somebody

takes me seriously. Drop in this evening and I'll perform
for you. Bring the Great Financier with you—that'll
please Faye no end.' Confidentially he added, 'That's why
she wanted to come back to the Caymans. She and Gideon
North seemed to have something going for them when we
had to leave—or Faye thought they had.' He chuckled. 'It
threw her mightily when he turned up last night with you
in tow, and when she heard you were staying in the
apartment alone with His Nibs she nearly exploded.' He
slid her a questioning glance.

But Susan wasn't to be drawn on that subject. She
laid her head back and looked up at the blue sky. 'Isn't
it a gorgeous day?' she said.

Out of the corner of her eye she saw his rueful grim-
ace. 'Point taken,' he murmured. 'Sebastian must mind
his own business. Accept my apologies, Miss—er——?'

'The name is Benton,' said Susan. She was almost
beginning to believe it.

'Accept my apologies, Miss Benton,' said Sebastian,
with such mock-humility that she couldn't help smiling.

'You may call me Della if you like,' she said. 'I seem
to remember that you've done that already.'

He hunched his shoulders over the wheel as if warding off a blow. 'You know how to keep a feller in his
place, don't you?'

'I hope so,' said Susan sweetly. It was fun flirting
lightly with this young man and held none of the dan-
gers of her relationship with Gideon North.

In George Town Sebastian stopped the car outside a
low building marked General Post Office. 'Come for a
drink—or coffee?' he suggested.

'Thanks very much, but no,' said Susan. 'I've got
quite a bit of shopping to get through.'

'And I suppose you'll be meeting the Financial
Wizard for lunch?' he enquired gloomily.

'Shall I?' she returned with a bright smile, climbing out of the car.

He sat with his hand on the wheel, his eyes fixed on her. 'Okay, I get the message. But just spare ten minutes for a drink first? There's a place down by the harbour where they do the most super sundaes and milk shakes—all fruity and mouthwatering. Please—I *did* give you a lift.' He pulled a pathetic face.

Susan relented. 'Ten minutes, then.'

'Great.' He looked round the busy road. 'This is one-way, I can't park here. Look, I'll just go on and leave the car somewhere. You drift down that street over there——' he pointed '——and I'll catch you up in a couple of minutes.' The cherry-red car disappeared with a leap foward into the traffic.

Susan crossed over and strolled along the street he had indicated, looking round with interest. She took an instant liking to the small town, with its graceful new buildings, their forecourts fringed with palm trees and trailing plants, bright green against the dazzling white of the walls. She supposed these were the commercial and financial offices, but it was difficult to think of this beautiful, sunbathed little town as being one of the money-markets of the world. How different from London, with its huge tower blocks darkening the sky-line, and its air of frenzied activity! Here, none of the buildings was more than three or four floors high, and everyone moved in a relaxed way, suggesting they had all the time in the world to spare.

She watched the passers-by with interest. Many were obviously tourists, but it was the ones who looked like West Indians that she studied. You could pick them out by the colour of their skin—from palest coffee to nearly black—and they moved with a lithe grace that was delightful to watch. Everyone she passed gave her a wide, friendly smile.

Further along the street were elegant stores, their windows a dazzling display of china and crystal, jewellery, watches, perfume—every luxury item you could imagine. The Cayman Islands were certainly a rich man's paradise—no taking home cheap souvenirs for the family from here. Susan's gaze lingered on a beautiful batik shawl in muted colours of orange and lemon yellow and mahogany brown.

'Seen something you like?'

She spun round to see Gideon North behind her, his enigmatic smile playing round his mouth. Her stomach contracted and she felt as if she were dropping down in a lift. 'Oh—hullo,' she said feebly. She passed her tongue over her dry lips. 'I—I didn't expect to see you.'

'I work here, you know,' he said, with a lift of his dark eyebrows, and she felt more idiotic than ever.

He put a hand at her elbow and drew her aside from the store entrance, to allow two large ladies with elaborately-coiffeured yellow hair and enormous sun-glasses to enter. 'I was looking out of my office window and spotted you arriving just now with friend Sebastian,' he said. 'I thought you might require rescuing.'

Susan was getting her breath back now, though she wished he would take his hand from her arm; the touch of his fingers had a weakening effect on her.

'Rescuing—of course not! We just happened to meet as I was leaving the apartment and Sebastian gave me a lift.'

'Just happened!' His tone was heavily sarcastic. 'I bet he was standing behind a bush watching for you.'

She turned wide eyes up to him. 'Rubbish! Why should he?'

'My dear girl! Have you looked in a mirror lately? As I mentioned before, you're a very lovely lady—and don't try to convince me that you don't know it. All the young hopefuls will be queueing up to escort you.'

She didn't at all like the look in his eye; what she saw there wasn't straightforward admiration, it was something much more dangerous.

'Sebastian is first in the queue this time,' she said lightly. 'He's taking me for a drink. I'm just waiting for him to park his car.'

Sebastian came rushing up then, weaving his way between the windowshoppers. 'Sorry to keep you waiting, Della——' he was panting a little '——I couldn't find a place to——' He broke off. 'Oh, hullo, Gideon.'

Gideon towered above the young man. In his light-weight silver-grey business suit with an open-necked white silk shirt, he looked very impressive indeed, a strong man, all firm muscle and taut skin, not an ounce of superfluous flesh on his body. Beside him the younger man looked almost flabby, with his curly fair hair and plump cheeks and his big clown's mouth. It wasn't fair, Susan thought, feeling sorry for Sebastian.

'Hullo, Sebastian,' Gideon greeted him pleasantly. 'Thanks very much for giving Della a lift. Very civil of you.' His hand still held her arm firmly. 'We'd all have a drink together, but I've got to take Della away now. We've got an appointment with Mike Green, to fix her up with some diving gear.'

Sebastian's face fell; he looked more like a doleful clown than ever. 'Oh well——' he mumbled. 'I suppose that's it, then.'

' 'fraid so,' said Gideon smoothly. 'Come along, Della, it's down this way. Be seeing you, Sebastian.'

Susan found herself being propelled firmly along the street, in the direction she had been going, and her last glimpse of Sebastian was of a forlorn figure standing gazing after them. 'Thanks for the lift,' she called back over her shoulder. 'See you this evening!'

His mouth pulled into a wide grin and he lifted a hand in salute.

Susan walked in silence beside Gideon for a few paces. She glanced up at the implacable profile of the man walking beside her. 'That,' she said coldly, 'was quite unpardonable. And very rude. Besides which, you were lying. How could you have an appointment when you didn't even know I'd be here?'

He kept looking straight ahead. 'We're making for the harbour,' he said. 'Mike's place is down that way. You'll find all you need there.'

Just as if she had never spoken! Her hand itched to smack that superior expression off his face and she was still seething with anger when they arrived at the dive shop. But once there she almost forgot Gideon North's nasty little ways as she looked round with enthusiasm.

It was all so much bigger and better-equipped than the teaching school in Devon. She saw at a glance that here was everything connected with diving that anyone could possibly need. A spurt of loyalty towards her old home made her add mentally that it *should* be bigger and better here, in this tropical island playground, where all the money was. Where self-assured, arrogant individuals like Gideon North would expect the best of everything. She darted a glance of dislike towards him.

He didn't see it. He was walking towards where a boy of about sixteen in denim jeans was sitting on a wooden bench, reading a paperback. He pushed it away and stood up when he saw Gideon. ' 'Morning, Mr North.'

' 'Morning, Jim. Mike around?'

'Sorry, Mr North, Mike went out with the boat.' The boy spoke in a soft, sing-song voice. 'Back about three, he said.'

H'm, thought Susan. So much for the story about the

appointment. He *was* lying.

Gideon clicked his tongue. 'Nuisance! Never mind, Della, you can fix yourself up with the basics and we'll load the stuff into my car and I'll run you back to the apratment.'

She said coldly, 'You may have forgotten, but I came into George Town to arrange about sending flowers to Uncle Ben.'

'So you did. We'll do that later. Now, take a look at these masks first. This sort of thing suit you?' He took a simple oval mask down from its hook.

Normally it would have suited very well, but Susan felt a strong urge to be as awkward as she could. 'I prefer one with a nose pocket,' she said calmly.

He showed no sign of irritation, merely took another one down. She held out her hand, but instead of giving it to her to try, he came closer and carefully smoothed her silky hair away from her face, smiling into her eyes as he did so, an urbane smile that made her look away quickly, her heart shaking.

'You're quite right, it's always as well to select a mask with care,' he murmured. '*Any* kind of mask,' he added with meaning. He held it to her face. 'How's that? Breathe in gently through your nose. No—*gently*.'

Beast! Susan fumed inwardly. He knew she was reacting to his closeness and to the touch of his fingers on her forehead as he held back her hair. He knew darned well that her breathing wasn't under complete control.

She moved away from him, shaking herself free. 'Let me do it myself,' she blurted.

He raised his brows and shrugged slightly, as he might do with a peevish child. 'As you wish.'

She took her time and tried several masks of different makes and sizes until at last she was satisfied. Then she spun out the business of choosing fins and the kind of snorkel tube she was accustomed to. Gideon leaned against the wall, watching her and saying nothing. She hoped her fussiness was annoying him, but if so he wasn't showing it.

'That's it,' she said finally.

He picked up a diver's knife in a sheath from the bench. 'You'd better have one of these. Never dive without a knife,' he added sternly, and she could have kicked herself for forgetting a rule that she knew perfectly well.

She said distantly, 'Shall I pay for these now?' She looked round for the boy, who had gone back to his paperback at the far end of the shop.

Gideon said, 'No, I'll see Mike about it myself later. And you'd better take a harness while you're here in case you want to try scuba. I keep spare air tanks at the apartment, but you'll have to let Mike put you through your paces first—I may not have time to teach you myself.'

Susan said nothing as she found a harness to fit. She would much prefer to dive with this unknown Mike Green—or anybody else—than with the chauvinist male standing beisde her now. She would well imagine how it would be with *him* as her diving partner. It would all be done as *he* said; he would criticise everything she did and she would be expected to follow him meekly wherever he led. He would never believe she was capable of making decisions or looking after herself.

'Right,' he said briskly, 'we'll go. You take the harness, I'll carry the rest.' He raised his voice to call to the boy at the far end of the long shop. 'We're taking this lot, Jim. Tell Mike, will you, and say I'll call in and see him about it—probably tomorrow.'

The boy looked up from his paperback, without rising. 'Okay, Mr North.'

'Lazy young devil,' muttered Gideon as they left the shop. 'The Cayman Islanders are quite delightful, but their trouble is that they haven't much sense of time.'

Quite a contrast, thought Susan, with his own clipped efficiency. He led her to his car, parked nearby, and stacked the gear inside. Then he took her to a store where there was a flowers-by-phone agency. Here Susan chose flowers for Uncle Ben and wrote a message—'Get well soon. Longing to see you. Love, Della.'

She could feel Gideon's eyes on her as she wrote and her hand shook. She couldn't bear to imagine his anger if he found out that she had been deceiving him. He wasn't a man who would take kindly to being made a fool of. She shivered as they went out into the hot sunshine.

'Anything else to buy?' He glanced down at her. 'You should be wearing sun-glasses, you know. The glare is very intense around midday here. Have you brought a pair with you?'

'No, said Susan. 'I've never worn sun-glasses—I've never needed them.'

He gave her an odd glance. 'Not even for winter sports?'

'No,' said Susan firmly. He would no doubt expect a rich's man's daughter to spend part of the year on the snowy slopes of Switzerland or Austria. But let him wonder—she didn't care. She added, 'I really don't want a pair, you know.'

'I think you should have them all the same,' he said, gripping her arm in a masterful way and steering her into a shop that displayed sun-glasses among the cameras and binoculars and movie projectors in the window. 'Go on, choose a pair. We don't want those melting wallflower-brown eyes to be put out of action, do we?' He smiled down at her mockingly.

She found herself resenting his attitude more every minute, but she had no choice. She could either comply or make a scene, for she could see he was determined to have his own way. Hastily she chose a pair of glasses that seemed to fit.

The girl assistant wrapped them. 'Ten dollars, please, madam.'

Susan half expected Gideon to come to the counter to pay for them, but he made no attempt to do so, so she took out the wallet that Della had given her and counted out ten dollar notes.

The girl took them. 'That will be two more dollars, please, madam.'

'I—I gave you ten dollars,' Susan stammered. The last thing she wanted was any unpleasantness in a shop, with Gideon standing looking on, but she was quite sure she had counted ten notes.

The pretty dark assistant smiled. 'You gave me ten *U.S.* dollars.'

Gideon lounged to the counter and tossed two notes down. 'That do the trick?' He put an arm carelessly across Susan's shoulders. 'Come along, Della,' he said in the warning tone of a man who is afraid the woman he is with is about to make a scene.

Outside again, she looked up at him stormily. 'What was all that about? I *did* give her ten notes, I know I did.'

'Ah, but a U.S. dollar is only worth eighty cents in Cayman currency. You'd better let me change your U.S. dollars, or you'll get horribly mixed up,' he added in the superior tone that riled her so much. 'Now, would you like a drink before I run you back to the apartment?'

'No, thanks,' said Susan distantly, averting her eyes. 'I'd prefer to go straight back.'

He shrugged and led the way back to where the car was parked. Susan walked beside him in silence. The sun was really dazzling now and commonsense told her it would be wise to put on the sun-glasses she had just been pressurised into buying. Most of the women tourists around—and many of the men—seemed to be wearing them. But that would seem like submission, and Susan had no intention of submitting to Gideon North in any way at all.

Back at the apartment he unloaded the diving gear and carried it through to a small annexe at the back of the building. It was very tiny, not much larger than a garden shed, but it housed a surprising amount of equipment, all neatly hung on, or arranged against, the wall. One glance told Susan that Gideon was a diving enthusiast—and was no doubt superlatively good at it. As well as the basic gear there were weightbelts and B.C.D.s—the kind of inflatable lifejackets to wear when diving deep. There was an inflatable dinghy and two surface marker buoys, also three tanks of air. Susan was impressed, but she wasn't going to let him see it—his masculine ego was quite sufficiently large as it was.

'I'll move my things over here,' he said, 'and you can have this corner.' She watched the tall, lithe figure of the man as he hauled items about, making room for what they had brought in, the powerful muscles of his arms rippling under the thin white shirt; he had long ago tossed the jacket of his suit aside in the car. There was a kind of controlled carelessness in his movements. He didn't seem to be exerting much energy, but everything was done with deft proficiency.

He straightened himself. 'There you are, all neat and tidy. I'll try to fix it so that I get some time off tomorrow and I'll take you snorkelling, for a start.' He turned to face her, which, as the room was so tiny, meant that they were standing only inches apart. 'You *do* understand, don't you, that you mustn't try using any of this stuff——' he waved towards the gear he had just stacked '——until I'm here with you?'

His nearness made her throat contract. She tried to move away, but her back was against the rubber dinghy on the wall. 'I understand that you say so,' she replied stiffly.

Gideon stood very still regarding her for what seemed a long time. Finally he said quietly, 'What's wrong, Della?'

She could let it go—or she could tell him what she was feeling. She swallowed hard. 'Nothing's wrong, exactly, except that I rather resent your attitude. Ever since we met in George Town you've been patronising me and treating me as if I were a child to be ordered about.'

He shook his head slowly, his eyes never leaving hers. 'I'm sorry if you got that impression, Della. I can assure you I don't look upon you as a child. I look upon you as a very lovely and desirable young woman. All I'm trying to do is to see that you're comfortable here and have a good time. What Ben asked me to do.'

'Ha!' She tossed her head. 'That's a good story! I suppose Uncle Ben asked you to—to seduce me too?'

His mouth firmed and there was a dangerous gleam in the gun-metal grey eyes. 'No,' he said slowly. 'That was my own idea. But I'm glad you've been thinking about it. Our little abortive session in my bedroom must have made quite an impact on you.'

'Oh, you——!' she gasped furiously, and her hand shot out to smack the mocking smile off his face.

But before she could make contact her arms were

held in a vice-like grip and she was forced back against
the rubber dinghy. 'Oh, no, you don't,' he said very
softly, and in the semi-gloom of the small, unlit room
his eyes held a dangerous glint. 'No woman attacks me
and gets away with it. I have my own method of
punishment.'

Susan felt her scalp prickle as she stared up at him,
and what she saw in his face made her shiver violently.
'Don't—please——' she whispered.

'Don't what?' His voice was silky, his grip didn't
relax.

'Don't hurt me—let me go——'

'Not just yet.' He smiled mockingly, slipping his
hands from her arms to her waist and thrusting her farther back against the wall, the length of his lean body
pressing against hers making it impossible for her to
move. She tried to struggle, to reach up to his shoulders
and push him away, but it was like pushing against
hard steel and she could only stare up into his cold grey
eyes with a kind of dreadful fascination while she
waited helplessly for his mouth to come down on hers.

He took his time over it, and when at last she felt his
lips close over her own a shudder passed through her.
She had vaguely expected his kiss to be brutal and
punishing, but his mouth moved gently, caressingly,
teasing her to respond.

She tried to keep her lips closed rigidly together, but
it was impossible. The sheer sensual impact of the man,
as his hands moved expertly over her body in its flimsy
covering, was having a disastrous effect on her nerves
and all thought was stifled in an uprush of an emotion
she had never known before. It was a red-hot flame
licking at her and she was powerless to quench it. Her
lips responded to his demands and her hands went up

to his shoulders, this time to lock themselves behind his head. She knew, with a small wave of shame, that she had been waiting for this ever since yesterday when he had wakened her from her dream with his lovemaking. As his kiss grew harder and more possessive her fingers fastened themselves in his hair, clutching it in a kind of frenzied desperation.

Suddenly he moved away and she was free, sagging against the wall, her knees shaking, her eyes wide and lustrous. He was breathing quickly and she felt a spurt of fierce gratification that he had been shaken out of his arrogant self-control.

But if he had it was soon over and his mask of assurance was firmly back in place. He stepped back, surveying her flushed face and tangled hair with a faint smile. 'That was a very pleasant little interlude,' he said smoothly. 'We must repeat it some time soon.'

She glared at him. 'I hate you!' she forced out between her teeth.

'Yes, I noticed that.' His eyes went to her mouth and to her utter chagrin he chuckled. Then he moved to the door. 'Sorry I can't stay to lunch with you. You'll find something in the fridge, no doubt. Or Owen will attend to you over at the restaurant, if you prefer. Tell him to put it on my bill,' he added.

'I'd rather starve than accept food from you,' she said wildly.

He was still smiling. 'Oh, I shouldn't take it as far as that. You've registered your protest—let's leave it there. We might even try a different approach from now on.' His eyes narrowed and his brows lifted thoughtfully. 'Yes, I'll have to work on that. 'Bye for now, Della, see you later this afternoon.'

She stood there shaking a little until she heard the

sound of his car die away in the distance. Then she
stumbled through the kitchen into the sitting room and
sank into a chair.

Her mind and her emotions were in turmoil. The way
Gideon North had treated her just now was callous,
uncalled-for, unforgivable, she told herself. And she
had enjoyed it, every nerve and cell in her body hunger-
ing for more. What was she going to do about it? she
wondered, in bitter self-contempt. She was in danger
from the man, but even more she was in danger from
herself.

She looked towards the phone as if it could somehow
save her from disaster. She wished Della would get in
touch—at least that would give her some idea of how
long she would have to stay and 'hold the fort' here.
She had half expected a call last evening, after she arrived, but of course Della would be madly excited about
Vic's tour, and about being with him. It was only natu-
ral that she should want to put off the fatal moment
when she would find out whether her Uncle Ben was
willing to back her up, or whether he was angry and
intended to get in touch with her father, in which case
her brief period of freedom would be over.

Susan sighed. She couldn't really blame Della for
grasping at her happiness, it was probably the first
chance she had had in her life. And the thought that she
herself had been able to help to give it to her made up
for getting tangled with the impossible Gideon North,
she told herself.

She wasn't in love with him, of course she wasn't.
What she had felt just now in the annexe was merely a
primitive, purely physical reaction to a man who was
suavely experienced in drawing that reaction from any
girl he chose. She wondered how many girls he had

made love to—dozens, she assured herself contempt-uously. He was the kind of man she had always thought of as utterly despicable. Which just went to show how your own body can let you down, if you don't watch it.

She would certainly watch it in future, she assured herself.

By now she was feeling calmer and she went through to the kitchen and piled up a plate with pears, pineapple and melon. She mixed a long, cold orange drink, and found a box of sweet biscuits. That would do for lunch. She carried the tray back to the sitting room and settled down beside the open window, gazing out at the glori-ous vista of blue sky and sunshine and the greenish streak of the lagoon beyond the fringe of sand. The trade wind blew a faint, refreshing breeze against her hot cheeks.

Suddenly she smiled. It was heavenly here and she was stupid to let anything spoil her brief chance of a stay in this paradise. She pushed everything to the back of her mind—Della, Vic, Uncle Ben, Gideon North—most of all Gideon North—and bit into a luscious pear.

There was a knock on the front door and almost immediately a movement on the patio outside the window and Sebastian's lanky form appeared.

'Hullo, sweetheart, I saw His Nibs' car go off and I thought I'd find you on your own. How about a swim later on? I've got to take Faye to lunch first and then she's going into George Town to get her hair done. Did you get your diving gear? I could show you our own wreck out there——' He waved a hand towards the reef.' How about it?'

Susan hesitated. 'I'd love to swim, but I'm not sure about diving. I'm rather out of practice.'

'You'll be okay with me,' Sebastian assured her. 'I'll

look after you. Nothing classy—just snorkelling around, you know. It'd be fun.'

It *would* be fun, thought Susan, her spirits soaring at the idea. There could be no possible danger in 'snorkelling around'. Gideon had been utterly unreasonable in forbidding her to use the new gear until he was with her. Why should she obey him?

'I'd love to come,' she said.

'Great!' Sebastian's wide clown's grin appeared. 'Down on the beach at around three, then, okay?'

'Okay,' said Susan.

He sketched a salute and disappeared along the patio and she leaned back in her chair, a satisfied smile on her mouth.

So you thought you could order me about, did you, Mr Gideon North? She bit into a crisp biscuit, her white even teeth crunching it pleasurably. She was going to enjoy herself this afternoon.

CHAPTER FIVE

SUSAN was enjoying herself. She finned lazily over the surface of the lagoon, face down in the clear green water, breathing easily through the mouthpiece of her snorkel, the taste of salt on her lips, the warmth of sun on her back, and the treasures of the underwater world beginning to disclose themselves to her fascinated gaze.

It was so *clear*! She'd read of diving in tropical waters, seen pictures, but the actuality was beyond her imagining. Now that she was wearing a mask and could see properly what lay below her, it was a revelation. She and Sebastian were swimming at the fringe of the reef, withing easy distance from the shore, and it was here that the sand ended and the coral began, the seabed showing subtle colours and textures, a myriad different forms that sent out fingers and fronds; sponge-like objects, pitted and grooved, in pink and gold and green; and tiny bright fish that glittered and twisted in and out of the coral formations.

Sebastian was amusing himself by diving below her and coming up on the other side, laughing and fooling about. He surfaced now, cleared his snorkel, and said, 'Come on, Della, why not dive down? I can show you how, it's quite easy. You only need to hold your breath for a minute or so.'

Beside him, Susan trod water easily. She didn't need showing how—she knew. But she wasn't going to admit it. She didn't want to get involved in diving with Sebastian because she was very doubtful about the way he was behaving. For one thing, he was hyperventilating before he went down, which was a thing she had been trained never to do. And for another, he was staying down far too long—she had a shrewd suspicion that he was showing off for her benefit.

'No, thanks,' she said. 'I'm quite happy paddling along for now. I love just looking down at the coral; it's like an underwater garden.'

'I could show you the wreck,' he urged. 'It's a very old one—just some bits and pieces of the ship lying around, but it's more exciting than just looking at the coral and the fish.'

'I don't think I want to explore a wreck just now. I'd rather have live things than dead ones.'

'Well, swim over with me and you can watch me go down to the wreck.' He was like a child, Susan thought with amusement. Watch *me*. Look at *me*.

'Okay,' she said. They ought to stay together anyway, and it was best that she should keep an eye on Sebastian. She didn't trust his technique at all.

He was quite a powerful swimmer, but she kept up with him easily as he led her to a spot where the depth of water increased and, looking into the clear green of the lagoon, she could distinctly see remants of heavy dark clumps of what looked like timber. The old ship must have foundered on the reef many years ago; a sailing ship probably. She had a quick picture of it, proud and beautiful, skimming over the dark ruffled water beyond the reef. And now—just a dead thing, black and encrusted, where sea creatures dwelt. She had no wish to investigate further; it would be like going sightseeing in a grave.

Sebastian pointed downwards, but she shook her head. He grinned at her, his wide clown's grin. 'Here we go, then!' The way he gulped in deep breaths made Susan wince, and then he launched himself downwards.

She kept her face in the water, breathing through her snorkel, so that she could see what he was doing. He was diving in and out of the remains of the poor sunken ship, playing with the fish that approached and stayed to watch, or swam away in silent protest. Now and then he waved up towards her gaily.

He seemed to her to be staying down much too long for safety and he was going deeper all the time. Susan's heart started to beat quickly as she ran over her rescue drill. The danger with breath-holding dives was, she remembered, of running out of oxygen, and the crisis crept up on you sneakily if you didn't take care to come up to breathe. You lost consciousness rapidly and became a drowning case.

She *couldn't* just wait and watch while he took risks like this. Taking a couple of good breaths, she dived down, finning skilfully. Thank goodness diving was like riding a bicycle—once you had learned you never forgot how to do it.

She had been right. Sebastian was scarcely moving; his body looked horribly flaccid. She grabbed him strongly round the waist and thrust upwards again, pushing until her leg muscles ached desperately with the unaccustomed exercise. Up, up, up. At last they broke the surface of the water and to her utter relief Sebastian began to cough and snort, and gulp in air. She pulled off his mask so that he could breath more easily and continued to hold him up with his head out of the water until the colour came back into his face.

At last she saw that his legs were moving and he was staying afloat by his own effort. He actually grinned at her. 'All right?' she asked anxiously.

'All right. I just lost my breath a bit.' His voice was a low croak.

Lost your breath! she thought shakily. You might very well have lost your life. 'Come on,' she said. 'Let's get back to the beach.'

He was swimming now—weakly, but at least he was getting along under his own steam. She stayed beside him, keeping a watchful eye on him, until they reached shallow water and began to wade out on to the sand.

It was then that she saw Gideon coming striding down the beach, a pair of binoculars slung round his neck, and his face like thunder.

'What the hell's going on here? I saw you from up there on the patio.' He glared at Susan and Sebastian, locked together with their arms round each other's waists as they staggered out of the water and collapsed in a heap on the sand. Susan took one look at his angry face and then lay back and closed her eyes. She had had a bad shock and suddenly she felt cold and clammy, even in the hot sunshine. Oh God, she thought, her inside churning, if she hadn't been there, if she hadn't somehow remembered all that she had learned way back in Devon when she took her diving tests, she might not have realised what was happening to Sebastian. He might even now be lying down there among that tangle of wreckage, cold and still. She shivered violently.

She heard Gideon mutter something, but it didn't seem to make sense. Then she was lifted in his arms and being carried up the beach and into the condo apartment. He took her straight upstairs and dumped her on the bed, tossing the coverlet over her. 'Stay there,' he ordered her tersely.

She opened her eyes. 'Gideon—wait,' she whispered.

He turned at the door. 'Sebastian—is he all right?'

'Perfectly all right, he was making his way home last time I saw him.' He moved impatiently to the bathroom and she heard water running into the bath. Then he returned to the bedroom and leaned over the bed to lift her again, but she struggled into a sitting position. Now that she was fully conscious she shrank from feeling his arms holding her. Even coming up the beach, when she was feeling definitely muzzy, she had had the most insane desire to clasp her hands round his neck and snuggle her face against his hard chest. Ridiculous! she told herself, disgusted with her own weak will.

'I can manage,' she told him, swaying a little as she got to her feet and clutching the edge of the bed for support.

'Don't be silly,' he said curtly, and scooped her up again. She was carried into the bathroom and lowered into a bath half full of blissfully warm water. Before she could sink down into it she felt his hands on her back releasing the fastening of her bikini top. He pulled it off and dropped it, dripping, on the carpet.

Susan slid down hastily, but to her embarrassment found that the water didn't quite cover her breasts, and she felt the heat rising into her cheeks as Gideon stood looking down at her, an unreadable expression in his cold grey eyes. And suddenly the whole situation struck her as quite ludicrous and she began to giggle weakly.

'Shut up!' he snapped. 'It's no laughing matter. I *told* you you mustn't dive, you stupid little idiot, and then you go out there and damn near drown yourself!'

Oh dear, she thought, he *had* got hold of the wrong end of the stick. But for some reason she couldn't try to explain that it wasn't her fault, that it had been due to Sebastian's childish showing-off.

'You told me I mustn't dive *alone*,' she reminded him. 'And I wasn't alone, I was with Sebastian.'

He gave a snort of derision. 'I wouldn't entrust a rubber duck to the tender care of Sebastian Lord as a diving buddy.'

Neither would I, thought Susan, but she didn't say it aloud. She said, 'How did you know where I was?'

'I came home early. I had an idea that you'd do something cussed, and sure enough when I got here I found you were missing and some of the gear we bought this morning was missing too. One look through the glasses showed me you and Sebastian along at the wreck and it was quite obvious that something was going wrong. Of all the bloody silly things to do, Della——!' He glared down at her furiously. 'Why couldn't you just do as I told you?'

That was what was enraging him, then. Not that she had nearly drowned—for that was what he obviously believed—but that she had disobeyed his orders.

It wasn't easy to be dignified, lying in a bath, topless, while he stood there staring down at her, but she did her best. She turned as far on her side as she could, presenting her back to him, and said coldly, 'Will you please go away while I dress?'

He didn't reply and she could feel the sudden tension in the small bathroom as he stood there, motionless. Then, abruptly, he went out and closed the door with a sharp click.

Five minutes in the warm bath worked wonders with Susan, both physically and mentally. By the time she had dressed—in jeans and a cream jersey top—and brushed her hair into shape after a good towelling, the effects of the shock had left her completely and she felt ready to face Gideon again.

She marched downstairs, her head held high, and found him in the kitchen. He handed her a beaker full of hot, sweet tea.

'Ugh!' She grimaced as she sipped it. 'I hate sugar in my tea.'

'This time you're going to like it, it's what you need.' He looked so threatening that she deemed it safer not to argue. She drank most of it and put the beaker down.

'Thank you,' she said, not very graciously.

She went into the sitting room and walked over to the open window, looking out. There were several groups of people on the beach, now that the day had got over its hottest period. Her glance travelled out further, fascinated as always by the sea. She had been half afraid that the lagoon might have changed, after what had happened, and taken on a sinister look, but of course it hadn't. It still looked calm and incredibly beautiful.

Gideon came up behind her. 'If you're thinking of repeating that little caper, you can forget it.' His deep voice was peremptory. 'I want you to promise me you won't go out diving when I'm not here.'

She resented his dictatorial tone. 'And what if I won't promise?'

He moved up beside her, taking her bare arm in a vice-like grip that felt as if it were breaking her bones. 'Then I'll have to use my own methods of persuasion,' he said grimly.

She gasped. 'Let me go, you're hurting me!'

'If you insist on behaving like a spoiled child, that's exactly what I shall have to do.'

Susan tried in vain to wriggle out of his grasp. 'You're a bully and a beast,' she spat at him, 'and I refuse to promise anything just because you tell me to!'

He released her arm and stood facing her, leaning against the window frame. 'And you're a selfish, spoilt little girl, totally uncaring about other people. You're a typical rich man's daughter—there are dozens of your sort around here.' His mouth drew into a hard, contemptuous line. 'God preserve me from rich men's daughters!'

So *that* was it! From the first moment they met he had placed her in some category, just as he might tell his secretary to file away a document in a special file. From that moment on, everything she did or said would be judged in advance. She glared impotently up at him. How she would love to tell him the truth, to taunt him with the fact that even his colossal arrogance could be dented. But of course she couldn't, because that would mean letting down Della and Vic.

But you wait until the need for this pretence is over, Mr Gideon North! She turned her back on him and walked to the other side of the room, picking up a magazine unseeingly. She was almost looking forward to seeing his utter surprise when he found out how wrong he had been about her—that she was just an unimportant typist and as far from being a spoilt rich man's daughter as she could possibly be. How he would hate to be proved wrong!

He came after her and took the magazine from her hands. 'Well,' he said, 'are you going to promise, or not?'

Susan raised her eyes and met his look squarely. She would not allow him to intimidate her, she would *not*. 'And if I do promise, why do you suppose that a selfish spoilt little girl would be likely to keep that promise?'

They looked at each other in silence for what seemed a very long time, but Susan wouldn't be the one to look away first. Even when his hand came up towards her face she refused to allow herself to flinch away. Let him strike her if he wanted to, it would just confirm what she wanted to believe—that he was a brute and a bully.

He touched her hair, where it was drying in little tendrils on her forehead.

'Unusual colouring you've got.' His voice was odd, not as if he intended a compliment but rather as if he were talking to himself. 'With hair as fair as yours one would expect you to have blue eyes, not brown.' He went on in the same musing tone, 'I think that was what struck me about your photograph, when I saw it at your home.'

The strange way he was looking at her, the touch of his fingers as they brushed against her cheek, was having a disturbing effect on her breathing. If she moved towards him a few inches her body would be touching his; if she lifted her mouth he would kiss her, of course he would. And then? The blood coursed wildly through her veins as his nearness worked its potent chemistry on her senses. Her heart was throbbing so heavily she thought its movements must show through the thin jersey that covered her breast.

He stood very still, just looking at her. It was as if he were waiting for her to make the first move—as if he were sure that she would. That thought brought sanity rushing back. She fixed a small ironic smile on her mouth. 'My photograph—oh yes, that was when you and J.B. made your nasty little plan for me.' She was pleased to hear the dry contempt in her voice.

He drew away from her, his expression hardening. 'I told you, it wasn't like that at all.'

She moved still farther, putting a low table between them. 'Of course you did,' she said indifferently. 'I'd forgotten. I think you said that the seduction idea was your own, didn't you? Brilliantly original!'

He took a step towards her and his eyes were like steel shafts piercing hers as he kicked the table aside. 'By God, you'll pay for that,' he muttered, and a thrill of primitive fear made her skin prickle. She'd gone too far, she thought in panic. You didn't needle a man like this—not if you were wise you didn't.

Gideon's hands gripped her arms and she closed her eyes as a shudder of pure sensual pleasure ran through her. When his mouth came down over hers, tense and demanding, she was powerless to stop her own response. For a long moment their bodies were locked together, straining against each other in mutual need. Then, abruptly, he put her away from him, his hands on her shoulders, his grey eyes fixed unreadably on hers. 'Who is seducing whom, I wonder?' he said softly.

There was a click of footsteps on the patio outside the open glass door and a husky voice said, 'Hullo, you two. I hope I'm not interrupting anything.'

Faye Lord stepped into the room, shattering the tension into a thousand particles. Susan's knees felt weak with reaction and she sat down quickly and composed her face as best she could. Let Gideon deal with this girl; she was his problem—if, indeed, she *was* a problem. And from the way he was smiling at her now, as if they were intimate friends, it seemed that he was really delighted to see her. Funny, thought Susan, last night he had been almost rude to Faye and now he was looking at her in a lazy, mocking way that seemed to hint at pleasures shared.

'Hullo, Faye, you're looking very beautiful,' he drawled. 'New hairstyle, isn't it?'

She laughed up at him, using her green cat-eyes extravagantly. 'All to celebrate our reunion, darling Gideon.' She touched her hair with delicate strokes of slender, scarlet-tipped fingers, smoothing the glossy black cap into its consciously-casual curves and spikes. 'So glad you approve.'

'Oh, I do indeed.'

She put a hand lightly on his arm and gave him a sultry look before she turned and drifted across the room towards Susan, the fine pleats of her white crêpe-de-chine dress swishing against delicately sun-tanned legs.

'And how is Ben's little niece? I just had to come and make sure that you were all right after your fun and games with my young brother.' She smiled winningly at a point on Susan's forehead. 'I really don't know what you two children got up to out there on the lagoon, but poor old Seb was quite tuckered out when he got in just now. I do so hope he didn't bother you with his foolery, my dear,' she added with a concern that sounded patently false to Susan.

'Oh no, nothing like that,' she murmured, and heard Gideon add dryly, 'Quite the reverse, I imagine.'

Susan's head jerked up and for a moment the tension was back between them. Faye glanced from one to the other and then went back and slipped her arm through Gideon's. 'Poor darling, it's quite a responsibility for you, isn't it?'

He looked down at her quizzically. 'What is?'

She waved her free hand vaguely in Susan's direction. 'Well, you know what I mean—having Ben's young niece to look after while he's ill. And such a pretty, attractive child too,' she added, with a bright false smile.

Susan stared. This Faye woman really was incredible —surely Gideon wouldn't be taken in by all this?

But Gideon, it seemed, was. 'Oh, I'm managing to

keep her in order,' he said comfortably, and Susan's hand itched to throw something at him, something large and hard.

Faye detached herself from Gideon reluctantly and drifted towards the window. 'I must go—I've let myself be lured into playing bridge with the Bensons. Rather a bore! But we'll see you this evening, shan't we? Seb tells me that Della has promised to come and hear him do his stuff with the guitar. He's positively swooning with joy at the prospect of showing off his talents. Do come for a meal—I'll get Owen to send something in. About eight? We'll look forward to seeing you both. 'Bye for now, then.'

With another intimate smile towards Gideon and a languid wave of her arm she had gone, the way she came in.

Susan sat waiting for Gideon to say something about what had happened. She didn't quite know what to expect, but *something* seemed indicated.

But all he did was glance at his watch and say briskly, 'I must be off. I'm expecting a call from Washington. I'm not sure what time I'll get back, but it'll be in time to take you to the party.' He stopped at the door and looked at her sternly. 'Now don't do anything stupid again. You'll be all right on your own?'

She smiled sweetly. 'I'll enjoy being on my own,' she said pointedly. He stared at her, frowning, then he muttered something under his breath and was gone.

The room was very quiet. It was as if a powerful motor had been vibrating and had suddenly been switched off. Susan sighed, shrugged, and wandered over to the bookcase. It was annoying to do as she was told by Gideon, but the fact was that she *did* feel like having a quiet afternoon, and that meant getting immersed in a good book.

She ran a finger along the contents of the bookcase. There were tomes on international banking practices, economics, company law. There were biographies, a sprinkling of modern novels and one or two paperback thrillers. But what she pounced on was a well-worn book on diving techniques. Delightedly, she pulled the sofa up in front of the window, curled up, and was immediately happily enthralled.

Time ceased to register until she was aware that the light was changing. She looked up and caught her breath. The sun was beginning to set and everything was steeped in gold. The sky was the pure yellow of a new wedding ring, the sea darker gold with a dazzling tracks of light zig-zagging down. Outside the window the drooping fronds of a palm tree were outlined in fine dark curving strokes against the sky, and in the lagoon the motionless masts of a schooner completed the picture of absolute peace. Fascinated, Susan watched until the sun sank, like an enormous half-apricot, below the horizon, and quite soon it was almost dark.

Suddenly the light snapped on and Gideon strode into the room, shattering the peace. 'All in the dark?' He eyed her jeans and casual top. 'I thought you'd be prettying yourself up for the party. Hadn't you better be getting a move on?'

He sank into a chair. If he'd been slaving in a hot office all afternoon he didn't show it—he looked cool and immaculate.

'I'm not sure I want to go,' said Susan, blinking against the light.

He jerked up in his chair and for a moment she thought she saw real alarm in his face. 'Not feeling ill, are you?'

She shook her head. 'No, it's just that——'

'Are you quite sure—no aches or pains anywhere?'

She raised her eyebrows. 'I'm feeling perfectly all right. If you're afraid that my—what did you call it?—my little caper out there with Sebastian has resulted in my getting the bends or something, please put it out of your mind.'

'Don't joke about it,' he said sharply. 'There's nothing funny about getting the bends.'

The sudden fury in his face shook her. 'I—I know,' she stammered. 'I was just remarking that you don't get the bends when you're snorkel diving, and that's all we were doing.'

He drew in a deep breath and said more calmly, 'I see you've been reading up on it.' He glanced at the book beside her on the sofa.

'I borrowed your book—I hope you don't mind.'

'Not at all,' he said rather stiffly. 'It belonged to my father. It's a little out of date, but the basic things don't change.'

He sat back and relapsed into silence for what seemed a long time, while Susan tried to think of something to say. He seemed all at once to have forgotten about her. His dark face had a withdrawn look, his eyes were half closed.

Then he opened them and said abruptly, 'Are you really keen on diving?'

She nodded. 'Yes.'

His mouth firmed. 'Right, then we'll go out together tomorrow morning. Mike seems to be booked up all week, and I'm not having you fooling around with Sebastian Lord again,' he added crushingly.

If he had phrased it differently—if he had said, 'Shall

we go diving together tomorrow? Would you like that?'
she would have been over the moon with delight. But
the way he had invited her—if you could call it an
invitation—put her off the whole idea. Much as she
longed to go diving, it wouldn't be much fun with
Gideon. She was out of practice and he would be a
severe and critical taskmaster, she was sure. She said,
'I wouldn't want to take up your time, I'm sure you're
very busy.'

He waved that away. 'We'll go tomorrow,' he said
again, and added, with what might have been a glimmer
of a smile, 'As Faye remarked, I feel responsible for
you, as Ben isn't here. Now go and get changed, there's
a good girl. Faye doesn't like to be kept waiting.'

She sat still, fuming, contemplating a blank refusal.
Then she noticed the gleam in his eye and remembered
exactly what had happened the last time she defied him.
Her head high, she turned away and marched out of the
room and up the stairs.

In her bedroom she stood looking at the plump blue
duvet on the big bed rather longingly. It was tempting
to crawl under the covers and not have to face that
awful woman Faye Lord again. If she said she was tired
and didn't feel like socialising Gideon would have to
believe her. He still thought she had had an accident
out there in the lagoon this afternoon.

On the other hand, it might create more problems
than it would solve. And anyway, she had promised
Sebastian, and a promise is a promise. Besides, she felt
a bit sorry for Sebastian, with a sister like his. Reluctantly she swished back the white door of the long wardrobe and surveyed the evening dresses that Della had
packed.

They were all of them luxury items, dresses any girl

would be thrilled to wear. She took the shell-pink one off the rail and held it up against herself, looking in the long mirror. It was a gorgeous dress, filmy georgette with glistening mother-of-pearl shoulder straps. It would look ravishing against sun-tanned skin, but it did nothing at all for her own pale arms and neck.

Faye, she was sure, would look glamorous, and beside that polished sophistication she would fade into insignificance in any case. Besides, she wasn't competing with Faye Lord for Gideon's attention.

Abruptly she spread the pink dress out on the bed and began to pull off her jeans and top.

She was on her way downstairs when the phone rang. Gideon called up, 'It's for you, Della. Vic something-or-other.' As she came into the room he gave her a dead-pan look and said, 'Your boy-friend, I presume.'

Susan's mind went blank. She took the receiver from him as if it were a poisonous snake. 'Hullo—Vic,' she croaked. 'Where are you?'

Vic's nice, humorous voice came over the line with reassuring normality. 'Still in Florida.' There was a guarded pause. 'Are you alone?'

Gideon was standing beside the drinks cabinet, one hand holding a glass, the other thrust nonchalantly into his pocket. He had changed into an evening suit of black pants and a pale amethyst silk shirt and he looked devastatingly handsome—and disgustingly self-satisfied.

Susan gave him a cold stare. 'No, Vic, I'm not alone,' she said pointedly. 'There's a friend of Uncle Ben's here, he answered the phone to you. His name's Gideon North,' she added as a clue. Della would re-cognise that name, even if Vic didn't. 'There's been an unfortunate hitch here,' she hurried on. 'Uncle Ben's ill in hospital in Texas. We don't know yet how serious it is, but he may have to have an operation.'

There was a low whistle from the other end of the line. Then Vic said in a lower voice, 'I guess we can't talk freely, then?'

'No, I'm afraid not.' Out of the corner of her eyes she saw Gideon saunter out on to the patio.

'Well, how are you making out?' Vic enquired, the question evidently loaded with meaning.

She improvised a code as she went along. 'Oh, fine—fine. This is a super place, and so long as Uncle Ben comes back safe and sound it promises to be a lovely holiday. I'm terribly disappointed that I can't see him and give him all the family news, though. That'll have to wait until he comes home, but I'm afraid it may be some time yet.'

She heard Vic's sigh of relief as he unscrambled the message. 'You're okay for the present, then? You can carry on?'

'Yes, I'm okay, Vic dear. You have a good tour and don't worry about me.'

A pause. She wondered if Vic had latched on to the soft, loving tone she was trying to inject into her voice. She said, 'How's the—the new member of your group getting along?'

Vic chuckled. He was quick on the uptake. 'Oh—Susan! She's grand, she's here beside me, only she thought it might be best for me to talk first. She says to tell you she's adoring every minute and she's finding our scatty existence entirely to her liking.'

That was splendid, it justified everything. 'Give her my love,' Susan said. 'And to you too, of course. We can't talk now, but send me an address I can write to as soon as you can.'

'I can give you one now,' he said. 'We'll be in Miami for the next week. Have you got a pencil?' Susan reached across the desk for a pad and pencil and wrote down the address he gave her.

'I'll write,' she said. 'Goodbye, my darling. I miss you——' she gulped '—all the time.'

She could almost see Vic look at Della and do a double-take as he put the receiver down.

Gideon came strolling back into the room and closed the glass doors. 'Insects get in at night,' he drawled. He looked her over from head to foot, in her ill-chosen pink dress. 'Are you ready?' He didn't try to disguise the irritated impatience in his voice. He couldn't wait to get to Faye, could he?

'Quite ready,' she said. She picked up her bag and swept before him to the front door.

'Della—just a minute.'

She stopped on the patio. The sky was black velvet now, the stars incredibly large and bright. There was a heavy flower perfume on the air. Gideon came up from behind her and she felt his hand close over her arm. 'We're not in such a hurry as all that,' he said, his voice softly mocking. Excitement rippled through her before she could even consider moving away. This man had a terrible effect on her senses. She stood still, knees quivering, waiting for him to move closer and draw her into his arms. She knew that if he did she couldn't resist.

He seemed to be waiting too. Then, after what seemed an age, he said, 'I thought you might like to hear the news about Ben.'

She let out her breath. 'Yes, of course, have you heard—I'd been wondering——' she jabbered.

He said in a detached sort of voice, 'I rang the hospital again from the office this afternoon. The surgeon saw him this morning and apparently there's some new treatment they're going to try. If it works they probably won't have to operate—which means that they'll send him home fairly soon to go on with the treatment at the hospital here. Good news, isn't it?'

The shock had sent her mind into a spin. 'Wonderful,' she said mechanically. Her voice shook a little. When Uncle Ben came back, it would all be over—the pretence, the lies. She could picture the cold contempt on Gideon's face. 'How soon?'

'They wouldn't say precisely, but I gathered it might be in a week or so.'

'That's absolutely splendid,' she said. 'I'm so glad.'

She would be glad, she thought, releasing her arm from Gideon's grasp as they walked along the shadowy patio. A week would give Vic and Della all the time they had asked for to make their plans. A week would see the end of her own necessity to act out a lie—that was good. And a week would also see the end of this spiky, false, frustrating relationship with Gideon North. That was good too.

Wasn't it? Yes, yes, yes, she told herself fiercely, it *was* good that he would get out of her life for ever and she would never see him again. Everything between them had been based on deceit and dishonesty (on her part; he had been straighforward enough, heaven knew!).

No good could come of a relationship like that. No good—ever. She marched along the patio ahead of him, the high heels of her satin shoes clicking defiantly on the paving stones.

CHAPTER SIX

'Whoa! where are you off to in such a hurry? We're here.'

Gideon stopped her in her tracks, one arm thrown carelessly about her shoulders, and turned her about. She drew away abruptly as a shiver passed down her spine at his touch. Oh, yes, indeed, it was just as well that this crazy episode in her life was going to end almost before it started.

He pushed open a door and called, 'Hullo—anyone in?' He sounded very much at home here.

A husky voice came from the room on their left. 'In here—come in, darling.'

The room was much the same size and shape as the one they had left, but there the resemblance ended. That room was a man's room, this one was all woman. The chairs and sofas were deep, with huge squashy cushions, all in muted shades of violet and aubergine. Satin curtains covered the long windows, concealed lights threw a rose-coloured glow over the room. An urn of great crimson blossoms flamed in one corner, exuding a curious, cloying perfume. Susan began to feel faintly smothered.

Faye was lying on one of the sofas, an empty glass on the low table beside her. She wore black, clinging pants and an almost completely revealing top in a jungle print. Her hair was a gleaming jet-black cap, sleek and sophisticated, with its points arranged like long birds' beaks against her forehead.

She got lazily to her feet. 'Hullo, you two, come in. Gideon darling, do something about drinks, will you— you know where everything is. Mix me one of my specials. Remember?' she added huskily.

She turned green eyes on Susan. 'Sit down, child. Delia, isn't it?'

'Della,' said Susan.

'Ah yes, Della, what a pretty name. And what a pretty dress. I always think the young look so sweet in pink. But we must do something about that pale skin of yours. Where have you been wintering, my dear? Iceland?' She laughed lightly.

Susan sat down, was received into the depths of the squashy cushions and sat up again. 'England,' she said. 'You don't get much of a sun-tan in London in December.' She looked across at Gideon, who was busy at the drinks cabinet. 'May I have a lime and lemon, please?'

She saw what might have been a faint twinkle in his eyes, but she was probably mistaken. 'Sure? Lime and lemon won't break down many inhibitions.'

Faye got up and drifted across to him. 'Don't tease the child, Gideon.' She laid a hand caressingly on his arm. 'Girls grow up early enough as it is without encouraging them.'

He looked from her to Susan, and now there was no doubt about the twinkle. '*Am* I encouraging you, Della?'

She looked at them, standing so close together, Gideon tall and handsome and assured; Faye gorgeous and exotic—a luxury item. They were from the same world, they spoke the same language, looked at things from the same angle. Especially their love-lives, she thought, with a stab of something that feld oddly like pain. She hid a small yawn delicately behind her hand and transferred her gaze to the urn of crimson blossoms, spilling out almost to the thick, oyster-pink carpet. 'I really haven't noticed,' she said with what she hoped sounded like total disinterest.

Faye sipped her drink delicately. 'And what kept you in London in the winter, my dear? A boy-friend?' she suggested roguishly.

'I was doing a job,' said Susan.

Faye gave a little scream. 'Don't tell me you're a career woman! They terrify me.'

Gideon brought Susan a glass and stood for a moment before he went to sit beside Faye on the sofa. He seemed to be watching Susan closely.

'Oh, nothing so grand as a career woman,' she said. 'Merely a common or garden secretary.'

'A secretary?' Faye's astonishment seemed genuine this time. 'You mean you work in an *office*?'

'I did,' said Susan, 'until quite recently.' It was a relief to be able to tell the truth for once, and let Gideon make what he liked of it.

'*Well!*' Faye shuddered delicately. 'There's no accounting for tastes. I should *die* if I had to work in an office.'

The topic was closed as Sebastian came into the room, wearing jeans and a blue and white spotted shirt. He made straight for Susan and sank down to the floor beside her chair, taking both her hands and looking up into her eyes, rather like a sad spaniel. 'I was half afraid you wouldn't come. Are you all right?'

She smiled down at him. 'Perfectly, thanks. And you?'

He pulled a wry face and she saw that he had worked out exactly what had happened in the lagoon this afternoon. 'Oh, I'm fine.' He hesitated. 'We got into a bit of a tangle, didn't we? We must try again tomorrow and make a better show of it. Yes?'

'No,' said Gideon definitely. 'I'm taking Della diving myself tomorrow. Just the two of us,' he added, fixing Sebastian with a steely glance.

Sebastian flushed and Susan felt sorry for him. She would feel sorry for anyone who came under the lash of Gideon's tongue. 'Oh yes, of course,' the boy said hastily. 'You're the expert, aren't you?'

'You could put it like that,' Gideon said dryly, and Faye leaned her head against his shoulder and gazed up into his face and murmured, 'Gideon's the tops at everything, aren't you, sweetheart?'

He smiled down at her and patted her hand and Susan felt like screaming. Was this the man who had said, 'God preserve me from rich men's daughters'? He had an original model beside him now and he seemed to be enjoying it, she thought with a deep wave of disgust.

Faye threw a glance of dislike at her brother, sprawled at Susan's feet. 'Can't you make yourself useful?' she said bitingly. 'Go over and tell Owen we're ready for food.'

Sebastian gave her a sulky look, unfolded himself, and went out of the room.

Faye clicked her tongue and cast her green eyes towards the ceiling. 'Lazy young layabout!'

'Oh, come,' Gideon said easily. 'He's not as bad as that. How about his music?'

'Music, is that what it is?' Faye raised perfectly-shaped eyebrows superciliously. 'That's only an excuse for not working. He's an absolute menace at home, drifting about. Daddy only sent him out here with me to get him off his back.'

Gideon's eyes narrowed teasingly. 'Cramps your style, does he?'

She stretched out an arm and fingered her way slowly up his shirt sleeve, across his shoulder and into the dark hair behind his ear. 'Not that you'd notice,' she murmured, gazing torridly into his eyes. 'Get me another drink, there's a darling.'

Sebastian was back in a couple of minutes. 'Food's on its way,' he said, sinking down on to the arm of Susan's chair.

'Don't loll about,' Faye said sharply. 'Pull the table out and put the chairs round.' She sighed. 'These condo apartments are so cramped.'

Sebastian burst out, 'Oh, shut up, Sis, you're always ratting on about something.'

Faye smiled at him viciously. 'Little boys,' she bit out, 'should be seen and not heard.'

Gideon brought her a drink. 'Now then, you two, no family squabbles. You're embarrassing Della.'

Susan wasn't embarrassed so much as disgusted. In her book you didn't invite people to dinner and behave like Faye was doing. But Gideon didn't appear to take exception to it. He was treating Faye like an amusing and lovable little kitten, all the more lovable for showing her claws.

'Don't mind them, Della,' he said tolerantly, and went to help Sebastian lift the glass-topped table out from the wall.

It was a heavy table and Susan noticed the ease with which he lifted, while Sebastian struggled with his end. Gideon placed the dining chairs two on each side. He looked suave and elegant and very much at home here, as if he had done this chore many times before. Susan wondered how soon after dinner she could plead a headache and get away.

Things improved marginally over dinner, helped by the fact that the main dish brought in by the smiling West Indian waitresses proved to be Owen's special—a turtle stew.

Gideon said, 'Della should know something about our Cayman main claim to fame, along with our banks and our postage stamps—turtles.'

'Turtles?' she echoed in surprise. It seemed somehow funny and unlikely.

He leaned towards her across the table, while beside him Faye toyed with her food in a bored sort of way. 'You see, Della,' he went on, his eyes alive with interest, 'our history is very different from the other West Indian Islands. It seems that in the beginning nothing and nobody lived here at all except the birds and the animals and—in the sea—the turtles. Giant green turtles—millions of 'em. There was nobody to catch them and there must have been a continuing population explosion. Then in the seventeenth and eighteenth centuries some of the bad guys who started to roam the seas around these parts were shipwrecked on the reefs and came ashore. They found the turtles were tasty to eat and that's how it all started. After that the pirate ships called here to stock up with turtles so that they could go on their merry marauding way with lots of fresh fodder in the larder. It stayed fresh because if you turn a turtle on its back it can't get away but it doesn't die—at least not for quite a time.'

Susan looked down at the delicious mess on her plate and pulled a face. 'How horrid of them,' she said. 'Now I know why the Mock Turtle couldn't stop sobbing.'

Gideon gave a guffaw of laughter, but Faye said in a superior tone, 'What *are* you talking about?'

'Surely you know your *Alice in Wonderland*?' Gideon teased.

Faye yawned. 'I don't go much for kids' stories,' she said, holding out her glass to him to be refilled.

Gideon caught Susan's eyes and smiled. 'I'll tell you the rest of the story some other time,' he said, and a sudden warm excitement ran through her as she thought how different he looked when he really smiled, without sarcasm or mockery. And she had a heady, triumphant feeling that in some way she had scored over Faye, just as if they were two women competing for the same man. Which of course was quite absurd, she assured herself.

After the meal was over Susan helped Sebastian carry the dishes into the kitchen, while Gideon made coffee in the percolator. 'Faye makes the most God-awful coffee,' he muttered, 'that's why I always take on the job.'

Faye didn't seem able to settle down. She wandered round the room, holding her coffee cup, pulling back the curtains, sliding open the long door, gazing out into the velvet, starry night. Gideon joined her there and they murmured together, laughing.

Sebastian disappeared and came back with his guitar. He pulled up a chair next to Susan and began to tune the lower strings, the sound throbbing and vibrating through the room.

Faye looked round and then up at Gideon, winding a silk-smooth arm round his neck, cuddling her cheek against his shoulder. 'Let's leave the children to their concert, shall we darling? Let's go and watch the moon come up.' Her glossy red lips were parted, her incredible lashes half lowered as she lifted her face to his in open invitation.

Why doesn't she swoon into his arms and make a real go of it? Susan thought tetchily.

She tried not to look, but her eyes returned with a horrid compulsion to the two by the window. Gideon's arms went round Faye's waist and he lowered his head and rubbed his cheek against her hair. 'Why not?' he said, and there was only a hint of mockery in his deep voice. This was for real, Susan thought, and suddenly felt hollow inside.

She watched them go out, appalled by the turmoil of her own feelings. Seb was watching them too.

He chuckled. 'What did I tell you? Faye's really on the scent now.' He strummed a few chords, giving a fair imitation of a hunting horn. 'Tan-tivvy, tan-tivvy, tan-tivvy!' he hollered.

Susan laughed immoderately. It was a good way of accounting for the tears that flooded thickly into her eyes.

Sebastian was silent, his hands resting on the strings. 'Do you mind?' he said rather awkwardly. 'About them?' He jerked his head towards the window.

She wiped her eyes, controlling her hysterical laughter with a great effort. 'Gracious, no,' she spluttered. 'Go on playing, do.'

He nodded, satisfied, and bent his tawny head over the instrument, plucking at the strings, improvising.

Susan lay back against the squashy cushions feeling as if all the life had been drained out of her, overwhelmed by sick misery as jealousy gnawed through her like a sharp-toothed animal. At last she had to admit the truth—that she was disastrously, totally in love with Gideon North.

After that the very last thing she wanted to do was to listen to Sebastian crooning love songs. Funeral dirges would be more in keeping with the situation, she thought, trying to see some humour in the way things were going.

He turned out all the lights but one—'To create the right atmosphere,' he grinned. It was sheer agony to sit there while the soft, plucked chords and sentimental little songs stole through the quiet room, and outside the sky was dark purple velvet and the stars were so bright and enormous that they looked as if they might come in through the window. She kept on wondering what those two were doing out there, and it was as if someone were carving her up into little pieces.

Sebastian went on and on, one song after another, and after a while Susan found she was listening with the front part of her mind.

'I liked that last one,' she said.

'Did you?' He almost purred. 'That's my favourite, too.'

'Sing it again,' she said, and when he had finished she smiled at him and said, 'It's very good, you know.' It was simple and yet with a catchy bit that stayed in the memory, so you wanted to hum it. She wasn't any judge from a commercial angle, but she was sure she had heard worse songs in the top twenty. It was called 'Love Me in the Morning'.

She said, 'You ought to get it published.'

Sebastian put down his guitar and grinned his sad clown's grin. 'Not a hope. You've got to know someone in the game, and then you have to find a backing group and have recordings done. Even that doesn't guarantee you a hearing. It's about as likely as winning the pools,' he finished wistfully.

He looked so forlorn that she wanted to comfort him. Perhaps it was partly to spite Faye, because Faye was so beastly to him and because she hated Faye as she had never hated anyone before in her life.

She said, 'I don't know if it would help, but I know someone—a singer with a group of his own. I couldn't promise anything, but if you've got a tape of that song I could send it to him, and he'd give you an honest opinion, I'm sure, if I asked him.'

Sebastian's eyes were alight. 'Really? Gosh, that'd be marvellous! What's his name?'

'Vic—Vic Wild. He's on a tour of the States and Mexico just now with his group.'

'Vic Wild? Yes, I've heard of him. He's up and coming, all right, and he sings my sort of stuff. Oh, Della—*would* you?'

'Yes, of course,' she said, and he hurtled upstairs and was back in seconds with a cassette tape. 'This is one I made last week—it gives you an idea. But of course,' he added quickly, 'it would sound quite different with a proper backing.'

'Yes,' she said. 'Vic would understand that.'

She let him go on a bit about how marvellous it was—that at last he'd get an opinion—not that he expected anything to come of it, of course—but at least he'd know whether it was worth going on trying——

At last she picked up the cassette and got to her feet. 'I'll send it off tomorrow. Would you mind terribly if I go now, Sebastian? I'm a bit tired.'

He leapt up immediately. 'Of course, you must be tired—after this morning and—and everything.' He paused. 'I'm sorry about that, it was stupid of me,' he said haltingly, and she squeezed his arm and said, 'Don't give it another thought.'

They walked back along the patio and stopped at the blue front door. Sebastian said, 'Thanks again, Della, I think you're the absolute tops.' He kissed her shyly on the cheek and said, 'This Vic—is he your boy-friend?'

Here it was again, and she was tired of hearing herself telling lies. 'Mmm, sort of,' she murmured vaguely.

'I was afraid of that,' said Sebastian, and watched her go inside.

She went straight upstairs and got into bed. Tonight she didn't even bother to lock the bedroom door. It wouldn't be necessary now that Faye had come back.

It was sheer black misery, lying in bed waiting to hear Gideon come in, scared stiff that he wouldn't come back at all that night.

But he did. It must have been around two o'clock when she heard his steps on the stairs and the door of his room closing gently. The relief was so enormous that she started tembling all over; she must have been lying stiff as a board for hours. But even then it was more hours before she fell at last into a heavy sleep.

The sun was pouring in through a chink between the curtains when she woke up. She didn't remember much at first, then she saw the cassette in its little plastic box with the green label lying on the dressing table, and that brought it all back and she groaned.

She lay back and let herself think about it. She must be raving mad to let herself fall for a man two days after she'd met him. But she admitted now that it had happened that very first moment when Gideon came towards her in the airport lounge, tall and dark and lean and handsome and utterly formidable. Only inbuilt habit had stopped her when he had tried to make love to her that first time. She wondered now what exactly would have happened if she hadn't stopped and fought him off. Would he have dropped her like a shot when Faye Lord turned up again? Of course he would.

Hadn't he made it very plain what he thought of her—a selfish, spoilt little girl. Good enough for a romp in the hay, probably, when there was nothing better in sight, but that was all.

Her eyes flooded with tears, but it was no good lying here howling. She had to get through the next few days until she got the All Clear from Vic and Della.

She got up and showered and dragged on cotton pants and a pink top. The face that looked back at her from the mirror was ghastly—great blue shadows under her eyes and white hollows in her cheeks. It was all very well having high cheekbones, but you needed to look your best to take full advantage of them.

She stared back at herself. 'Where have you been wintering, my dear? Iceland?' She mimicked Faye's husky voice and pulled a horrible face at herself. Then she found she was going to start crying again, so she quickly dabbed on some of Della's expensive foundation and blusher and went downstairs.

Adèle was flicking round the sitting room, moving in little dancing steps and crooning a French song. She grinned widely. 'Good morning, miss, you 'ad a nice sleep? Mr North 'as gone out. He says you were still sleeping and not to disturb you. He will come back later on to take you swimming.' She gave Susan a knowing little smirk. ''e is vairy nice, Mr North.'

'Very nice,' agreed Susan without emotion.

Adèle smoothed her duster slowly over the top of the polished table. 'Miss Lord, she like to know everything. She ask me what goes on here. She ask me yesterday, but today I can tell her that Mr North's bed was not slept in last night.' The sloe-black eyes danced with mischief.

Susan jumped. 'What did you say?'

'I think it is lovely,' beamed Adèle. 'You and Mr North, you are so beautiful together, 'im so dark and you so fair. Miss Lord—pooh!' She swept a crumb off the table with a contemptuous flick.

Susan said hurriedly, 'Adèle, you mustn't tell Miss Lord anything of the sort. Besides, you're quite wrong. Mr North *did* sleep in his own bed last night.'

'Come and look,' Adèle said simply, and led the way upstairs.

Susan followed, in rather a daze, and they stood together in the doorway of Gideon's bedroom. 'You see?' Adèle slid her a sly glance.

Gideon's bed was smooth and creaseless, the ivory silk cover pulled up over plump pillows. Not a wrinkle anywhere.

'He—he must have made it himself, then, before he went out.' Susan said weakly. It was quite ridiculous how standing here looking at Gideon's bed had made the blood run up into her cheeks.

Adèle cast her eyes down. 'Ah yes, of course, I would nevair 'ave thought of that. He 'as nevair done so before,' she said with great solemnity. Then she looked up with a wicked little grin. 'You look vairy pretty when you blush, miss.' She folded her duster. 'I 'ave finished—I go now. See you tomorrow, yes?'

In the beautiful white kitchen Susan made herself a mug of coffee, cut off two slices of rather stale bread and stuck them in the toaster. She ate them prowling round the kitchen; she was too jittery to set a table and eat breakfast properly. What was Gideon up to? She couldn't make any sense out of it. If Adèle had been telling the truth when she said that Gideon had never made his own bed before—and there didn't seem to be any reason why she shouldn't tell the truth—then why? There seemed to be only one answer: that he wanted to get the news through to Faye Lord next door that he and 'Della' only required one bed between them. But why should he want Faye to think along those lines? Especially when he'd stayed with Faye until all hours last night.

She didn't want to start remembering last night, so she went into the sitting room and wrote a letter to Vic and Della.

There wasn't much new to tell them that she hadn't told Vic on the phone, except that Uncle Ben would probably be coming home sooner than they had thought at first. 'Perhaps in a week,' she wrote. 'Will that give you two enough time to sort things out? I think I'd better write to him at the hospital and explain things—I'd hate him to get a shock when he gets back and finds me here instead of you, Della. It might set him back as he's been so ill. I promise I'll put it all very tactfully.'

She told Vic about Sebastian and his music. 'I offered to send you a tape of his songs. I thought they were rather good, but of course I wouldn't know. Would you listen to the tape as a favour to me, Vic, please, and give him your opinion. All he expects is just a Yes or a No. I know it's rather cheek, but Sebastian is a nice boy and I'd like to help him.'

She finished, 'Have a lovely time, darlings. I'm really enjoying myself here, it's a heavenly place. I'm hoping to get some diving in the incredible lagoon—it's something I've always been keen on.'

She put a P.S. at the end. 'Did you get a shock when I swooned over you on the phone, Vic? As you'll have gathered, this Gideon North man is in the picture here. He shares the apartment with Uncle Ben and is a bit of a little Hitler, but I'm managing to cope with him. I haven't been able to tell him the truth, though, because I couldn't be sure he wouldn't blow everything sky-high. Apparently he knows Della's father. He sort of assumed you were my boy-friend when you rang up, so I let him go on thinking it. Hope you don't mind.'

She found a strong envelope in the desk pigeonhole, packed up the letter and the cassette and addressed it to the hotel in Miami. Then she put it into her handbag and wandered across to the window.

The sea looked unbelievably beautiful this morning, the lagoon smooth and inviting, with the darker ridge showing the reef below, and the blue, blue water beyond. She'd read about 'diving the wall' on the far side of a coral reef, where the sea goes down to un-imaginable depths and exotic fish glide in and out of dark caves. But that wouldn't be for her. Gideon wouldn't let her do that sort of diving, and she couldn't go alone.

Gideon. Her inside cramped painfully at the very thought of him. She tried to work up anger about the bedmaking ploy – he was devious and it was a con-temptible trick, she told herself. Perhaps anger would help her to get over this awful yearning. She picked up a magazine and tried to concentrate on an article about climbing in the Himalayas.

It was nearly eleven when Gideon came in and im-mediately the room was full of his dynamic, masculine presence.

He said abruptly, 'Aren't you ready? I left a message with Adèle.'

Susan looked up from the magazine she had been pretending to read. 'When you were so late I thought you'd probably changed your mind,' she said coolly.

'Of course I hadn't—I said I'd come.' When she didn't get up he came and stood towering above her chair. 'What's up, Della? Sulking about something?'

That supplied the spark she needed. She stood up and met his eyes accusingly. 'Why did you make your own bed this morning?'

'Make my—what the hell——?' His expression changed and a faint grin pulled at his mouth. 'Well, why not? I was brought up to make my own bed. We all had to, at school. I often make my own bed.'

'Adèle doesn't think you do. In fact, she said you never do.'

He shrugged. 'Does it matter what Adèle thinks?'

'Yes, it does,' she said hotly. 'She thinks the worst about you and me and she's gone off hot-foot to spread the news to Miss Lord, next door.' She saw the bland satisfaction in his face and rushed on, 'I suppose you enjoy playing one girl off against another. Well, I think it's a lousy game and please leave me out of it in future.'

'Afraid the boy-friend will find out?' he mocked.

'Oh, shut up!' She flounced away and went out on to the patio.

He came after her. 'I've come back specially to take you diving,' he said in a long-suffering voice, 'not to listen to a nagging female. Do you want to come or not? If so, I suggest we get our gear and get moving.'

Here we go again, thought Susan mutinously. I have to be seen to be obeying him, I bet he enjoys that.

It was maddening, but this was one proposition that she couldn't refuse. 'I won't be two minutes,' she said, and ran upstairs.

She pulled off jeans and top and found the most businesslike of the bikinis—a black one—and got into it, pausing for a moment to glance at herself in the long looking-glass with a certain amount of approval. Could she have collected the faintest of creamy tans in just one day, or was it imagination?

Over the bikini she pulled on a pair of white cotton pants, because of the sun, and a white silky blouse. Into a beach bag went a towel, a bottle of sun-tan lotion, a comb, and the sun-glasses that Gideon had made her buy. At the last minute she remembered the letter to Vic and tossed that in too. She must be sure he received it before they left for Mexico.

Gideon was waiting in the car when she arrived downstairs. He leaned across and opened the door for her. 'I've packed everything,' he said.

'Aren't we going to swim from the beach here?' she asked him, looking across to where a few brown bodies were lying out in the sun.

His hand was already on the gear lever. 'I have my own favourite spots,' he said. 'Hop in.'

As they moved off along the condo service road Susan said, 'Could we possibly stop on the way to post a letter?'

'Is it stamped?'

She shook her head. 'I didn't know how much it would be. It's a small parcel really, not a letter.'

He clicked his tongue irritably. 'Oh well, we'd better go up north to swim instead of the place I intended to go to. We can post your letter from Hell.' He pulled the car round left into the road and it roared away.

Had she heard right? 'Post it *where*?' she asked faintly.

'Local joke. West Bay's a little town up in the north of the island and Hell's a sort of suburb of it—so-called because of the black spiky rocks there. The tourists love sending picture postcards home to their relatives post-marked Hell. You know—"Wish you were here." Very funny!'

Susan glanced up at the austere profile, the cold grey eyes fixed on the road without a glimmer of a smile. He *was* in a sour mood this morning!

She said, 'I thould think you often get bored here, don't you?'

He shot a quick, raking glance at her before returning his attention to the road ahead. 'One can have too much of a good thing. A paradise island is all very well, but I've been here nearly three years now and I certainly shan't be sorry when my stint's over and I get back to old grey, dirty London.'

After that they drove in silence until they reached a fork in the road. Gideon nodded towards a sign saying Mariculture. 'Turtle farm,' he said. 'Another of the local attractions. I'm told they have as many as seventy or eighty thousand green turtles breeding there, in various stages.'

'Gosh,' said Susan, amazed. 'They must be awfully fond of turtle soup.'

It wasn't a very good joke, but he might have smiled, she thought glumly. It certainly didn't promise to be a very hilarious outing.

A few minutes later the car pulled up. Susan looked out and saw a wooden board stuck in the ground, on which was printed in large black letters: HELL, and underneath: Postal Agency. At the end of a short path, bordered with flowering plants, was a green clapboard hut with a corrugated roof.

She smiled. 'It looks much too pretty for Hell.'

Gideon said, 'You'd better let me post your letter for you. It'll probably be crowded inside and I'll get attention quicker than you could.'

Yes, she thought, he certainly would. She could just see him cut through the crowd like a speedboat through the sea, and the waters would part to let him through. She giggled at the idea.

'Come on,' he said impatiently, holding out his hand.

She took the package from her bag and gave it to him. 'What's inside?' he asked. 'Is it dutiable?'

'I—I don't know. I hadn't thought of that. It's a cassette tape.'

He glanced down at the address. 'I suppose the boy-friend can't get along without a recording of your lovely voice,' he said nastily. He got out of the car and strode down the path.

Beast! fumed Susan. Horrid, sarcastic beast. How could she possibly have thought she was in love with him?

He was back very soon. He climbed in to the car again and Susan asked stiffly, 'How much did it cost? I'll repay you when we get back.'

'Don't bother, I'll treat your boy-friend to the recording.' He looked down at her, smiling broadly. 'It's the very least I can do as I have the original in my possession just now.'

He started the engine and then, his hand on the gear lever, he added in a lazy, provocative drawl, 'I just hope he knew what he was doing when he let you out of his sight.'

The roar of the engine saved her from replying. As the powerful car moved away she laid her head back and the sun was hot on her cheeks. The breeze flipped her hair away from her face in a pale gold drift across the back of the seat. She looked enchanting—a pretty girl enjoying a carefree holiday with a handsome man at the wheel beside her.

But inside she was churning painfully. Gideon's

mood had changed, and with it the whole mood of the day. Suddenly the hours ahead seemed to be quivering with excitement; to be full of a dangerous, reckless, intoxicating promise.

CHAPTER SEVEN

A MILE or two on Gideon parked the car in a small clearing off the road. He switched off the engine and sat back. Then he said, 'I think I must clear up that bed thing that you were asking about earlier on. I'm sorry about involving you, Della, I really am, you must believe that. I wouldn't have done it if I hadn't been desperate.'

Susan's head jerked round. 'Desperate?'

'Yes. You see, Faye hears the tinkle of wedding bells and I had to get it through to her, as gently and tactfully as possible, that I wasn't interested. That I was otherwise occupied—with you, in point of fact. I knew Adèle would draw her own conclusions if she found that only one bed had been occupied last night and would pass the news on to Faye.'

Susan exclaimed, 'God, you're devious, aren't you? Why couldn't you just have given her a brush-off without dragging me into it?'

He looked wry. 'My dear girl, you don't know what you're talking about. Faye Lord's father is one of my company's most cherished clients—influential too.'

'And she might harm your career?' Her lip curled. 'What a shame!'

He sighed. 'You may not believe it, but I happen to have a certain loyalty to the concern I work for and represent.'

Yes, she thought, looking at his thin, strong face, you

139

probably are loyal to your company. It was a pity the code of morals didn't extend to his private life. He would use women just as he liked and take whatever he could get—he had made that plain already.

Probably the women in his set had much the same attitude towards casual lovemaking: enjoy it and forget it. But that wasn't the way she looked at it. She guessed she wasn't a casual sort of girl. That being so, it was strange that she should feel this bubbling sense of elation because he didn't want Faye.

He turned his head towards her. 'Am I forgiven?'

She shrugged, 'It's done now.' She couldn't leave the subject alone. She heard herself say, 'Sebastian thought you were going to marry Faye.'

Gideon smiled grimly. 'Did he now? Never in this world!'

'She's very attractive.'

'Possibly. She's also self-centred and as tricky as they come. She'd lie her head off without a qualm to get what she wanted.' He was silent, looking out at the dense green foliage in front of the windscreen. Then he said quietly, 'I grew up in a happy home. My parents had a good marriage—honest, trusting, understanding. I'd never settle for less.'

His expression changed and he laughed. 'When I meet a girl who can tell the truth I'll consider making an honest woman of her. Now, come along, let's get the gear unloaded.'

He had packed their diving equipment in the back of the car. He took it out now and said, 'We're only snorkelling today. I want to see how you shape before I let you loose with an air tank. Oh, by the way, I took the precaution of bringing some drinks along. I hope they'll keep cool.' He held out a couple of vacuum flasks to

Susan. 'Can you take care of these while I carry the rest.'

He led the way through overhanging bushes and low trees on to a rough path. Susan followed thoughtfully, her mind on the conversation they had just had. But when they came out at last into a tiny secluded cove she could think of nothing but the delight of the scene in front of her.

'Oh, it's lovely!' She drew in a breath of pure pleasure. 'Like having our own little desert island.'

Flowering bushes enclosed the cove on both sides, almost down to the sea, with tall palm trees dotted here and there in the background, and straight ahead the water glittered in the sunlight.

Gideon looked up from unpacking the diving gear and grinned. 'We aim to please.'

He looked quite different from when they had started out—more relaxed, less aggressive. Perhaps he had been feeling guilty about the way he had used her to discourage Faye. It didn't seem likely, but it was possible. Susan's spirits rose.

A fallen tree trunk, bleached white by the sun, lay across the sand and Susan sat down on it and started to pull off her white silk blouse. A large seabird swooped and landed, and stood motionless at a short distance, one unblinking yellow eye fixed on her.

'Hey, go away,' she laughed. 'Where are your manners?'

Gideon looked up and his eyes passed over her slowly as she scrambled to her feet, the sun kissing the lovely curves of her body in its minuscule black bikini, the breeze lifting the pale gold hair from her forehead. Then, deliberately holding her gaze, he said slowly, 'His manners may be a little off, but his taste is all that could be desired.'

Susan bent quickly to pick up her face-mask, hiding the flush that ran almost painfully into her face. Her fingers shook as she tried to fasten the strap.

'Let me fix it for you.' Gideon came close, too close for her peace of mind, and as she felt his hand brush her cheek her heart began to thump with heavy beats. She stood very still, holding her breath.

He secured the strap and his hand slid down her cheek to her neck, closing round it, squeezing gently. In the sunlight his eyes were brilliant, like diamonds. He said ruefully, 'I seem to have the greatest difficulty in taking my hands off you, Della Benton.'

She gasped and wriggled out of his grasp. 'I thought,' she said primly, 'that you said you came home specially to take me diving.'

He let her go. 'Okay, okay, you win.' He picked up both their pairs of fins and started down to the edge of the lagoon.

Snorkel diving with Gideon was quite a surprise. Susan had thought he would be impatient and peremptory, barking out orders, but instead, all he said was, 'Stay close to me and on no account go deeper. And come up at once when I signal. Now—ready?'

It was like riding a bicycle, you never forgot. She remembered the drill: Don't overbreathe. If your ears pop, hold your nose and blow out gently through your mouth. Above all—slow, slow, slow, to conserve your oxygen. On the first dive she didn't see much, she was too busy concentrating on her technique. But after that confidence returned and after the third time down she found that Gideon was allowing her to go a little deeper and stay down a little longer. All the time she was very conscious of his tall, lithe body close to her as they glided together through the clear blue water, finning lazily in unison, and she knew he was sharing the pleasure with her, and was ready to help at a moment's notice, if she needed help.

The underwater scene was pure magic, a bewildering symphony of colour and form. Coral formations in every shape imaginable, from narrow tubes sprouting upwards like organ-pipes to great boulders from which floated lacy trees and weeds that waved and swayed in the eddying current. It was a fairyland of pink and blue and green and cream, and the tiny fish were everywhere, darting in and out of the encrusted rocks.

At last, as they surfaced for the seventh time, Gideon pushed his mask back on to his forehead and said, 'That's enough for now,' and it never occurred to Susan, this time, to disobey.

The sun was almost directly overhead now, but there was a mercifully cooling breeze. They lay back in the shade of a tree and were dry almost at once. 'Oh, that was marvellous,' Susan breathed. 'Absolutely marvellous!'

Gideon pulled out the flasks and poured her a drink, fruity and tingling and deliciously cold. 'You're quite a water-baby, aren't you? Why didn't you tell me you could dive like that?'

She felt a quick rush of pleasure at his praise. 'I think the stock answer is that you didn't ask me. You just took it for granted that I was a novice.'

'You're no novice,' he said. 'You've done scuba diving, too—got a certificate?'

She nodded. 'B.S.A.C.'

'That's fine. Mike will welcome you with open arms—he'll take you out in the boat while I'm away.'

'You're going away?' It was like a little pain shooting through her.

'Yes—a damned nuisance, but there it is. One of our biggest clients is starting up a colossal building project in Tobago and I've got to go over there to vet it and see if our money's safe.'

'H-how long will you be away?' Susan choked a little on the question and turned it into a cough.

'Dunno,' he said, trickling a handful of sand through his fingers. 'I'll try and get through inside a week. We must go diving again together. Not just in the lagoon. There are some splendid places out beyond the reef— you get into really deep water there.'

She looked at him as he leaned back against a tree— at the planes of his face, the slight hollows beneath his cheekbones, the faintly etched lines running from nose to the corners of his level mouth, his dark coppery hair rumpled and glistening where the salt had dried on it, and suddenly her pulses began to throb. I'm in deep water already, she thought.

He asked, 'What exactly did happen when you were swimming with Sebastian yesterday?'

Susan flushed and looked away. 'Does it matter now?'

Gideon said slowly, 'I think I can make a pretty shrewd guess.' There was a long silence and then he said, 'It seems there are quite a number of things I've taken for granted about you.' He put down his drink and moved closer to her, propping himself on one elbow, the long length of him stretched out on the sand. 'Too many altogether,' he added in a low, husky voice.

She sipped her drink, her heart beating heavily, terribly conscious of a magnetism that was drawing her down towards him. She ought to get up, to say something that would snap the tension between them, but her limbs refused to move, her voice was soundless in her dry throat.

After what seemed an age he stretched out and took the drink out of her hand and held the beaker upside down. Not a drop came out and he smiled and tossed it aside. Then, gently, he put his hands on her shoulders, pushing her down into the warm sand.

'God, you're lovely,' he muttered.

His face was close above her now, shutting out the sun. She felt the weight of his body and was helpless against the tense hardness that pressed down on her. She longed for the touch of his mouth on hers as she had never in her whole life longed for anything. Waiting was exquisite agony.

'This fellow——' he muttered, 'this chap Vic you say you're in love with—are you going to marry him?'

Susan shook her head from side to side.

'He's—tied up elsewhere, is he?'

'Yes,' she gasped. 'Yes, he is.'

She couldn't wait any longer. She reached up and pulled his head down until his mouth rested on hers. Her lips parted and she gave herself up mindlessly to the ecstasy of his kiss. Shivers of delirious pleasure passed over her as his hands moved across her shoulders and down to her waist and over the rounded contours of her hips. She was achingly conscious of the soft yielding of her breasts against his hard chest. The straps of her bikini top had slipped and he pulled them off still farther, trailing his mouth down to rest softly, excitingly against the swelling curves which the narrow top had covered.

Wave after wave of warm, sensual pleasure coursed through Susan's body as his hands roused her expertly to new, unknown delights. She could feel the heavy beating of his heart joining with her own. Her fingers wound themselves in the thick hair at his neck and she groaned and arched her back as desire mounted in her. She was released from thought, from fear, a prey to needs as basic as human life.

Then, abruptly, his head lifted and she heard him swear softly, savagely, close to her ear. She felt him move away from her, but her senses were swimming and for a moment she couldn't take in what was happening. She sat up, shivering, dazzled by the glare of the light splintering the branches of the tree. Gideon had rolled away and was sprawled on the sand, leaning back on his elbows, his long legs stretched out before him, dark brows drawn together in an expression of pure rage.

Susan followed his look and saw a man dragging a dinghy up on to the beach, not twenty yards away from them. Several small children tumbled out of the boat, shrieking and falling over each other in the shallow water.

One of them, a little girl of about three, stumbled up the shelving sand towards Susan and Gideon, holding a large red inflatable ball over her head, chuckling gleefully, preparing to launch it at them.

'A desert island, did you say?' Gideon's furious comment reached Susan's ears. 'More like Children's Corner at the Zoo!'

The man came running and scooped the child up under one arm. He glanced apologetically at Gideon. 'Sorry, chum, we'll move further along. Come here, Adam—Charles—Penelope—come *here*, you little devils!'

The party straggled along and established itself at the other side of the small cove.

Gideon sat silent for a minute or two, his head buried

in his hands. Then he looked up at Susan. 'The Cayman Islands are the most uncluttered part of the Caribbean, and this cove is one of the more remote spots in the Cayman Islands. And yet they had to come here.' He looked up at the sky. 'Maybe your guardian angel was watching over you. Come along, we'd better move.' He began to throw their diving gear together.

In the car Susan was very quiet. If that party hadn't arrived she would have let Gideon make love to her, and it would have meant almost nothing to him. A lonely spot—a girl—a few minutes' pleasure. But to her it would have been unforgettable, something that she would have to live with and yearn for in the weeks and years ahead, when he would have gone out of her life.

For there couldn't be any future that included herself and Gideon, together. There was too much against it. She heard again his voice saying, 'When I meet a girl who can tell the truth I'll make an honest woman of her.'

And she had lied to him and tricked him from the first moment they met. She went cold as she realised that very soon he would have to know the truth about her.

Maybe, she told herself, it was a merciful thing that her guardian angel had been watching over her. She would have to try to believe it.

Gideon drove straight into George Town and parked outside the dive shop where Susan's equipment had been bought. As soon as they appeared a redhaired, stocky man with a battered, cheerful face came across the shop. 'Hi, Gideon old son, how goes it?' He clapped Gideon on the back.

Susan wouldn't have thought that Gideon was the

kind of man who would tolerate being clapped on the back, but she was wrong. 'Hi, Mike,' he returned, and pushed Susan forward. 'I've brought you a surprise gift. Ben Caldicott's niece—she's over on a visit. I told you about Mike, Della, there's nothing he doesn't know about diving.'

Mike held out a large hand and as Susan's was enclosed firmly in it Gideon added, 'Della's dead keen on diving, Mike, and she's quite a gifted lady, B.S.A.C. certificate and all.'

Mike surveyed her with increased interest. 'Great,' he said.

'Now look, Mike,' Gideon continued. 'Ben's still in hospital and I've got to go off to Tobago for a few days, so I'm counting on you to keep Della happy— find room for her in your dive boat, maybe.'

'Sure,' Mike beamed happily. 'As much as she wants. I've just had a cancellation. Family from Boston booked with a son and daughter, and now the son's dropped out—gone off to Europe. Della can come in in his place. They're all experienced—been here the last three years. Nice people.'

Gideon looked at Susan and then back at Mike. 'Just so long as it's the *son* that's gone off to Europe——' he said meaningly, and Mike grinned broadly and said,

'Nice work, chief, I get the message. How about tomorrow morning, Della? I'm taking the Fergusons out at ten.'

'She'll be here,' Gideon promised for her. 'Her gear's in my car outside, Mike. Will you take care of it for the moment?' He went to get it.

Outside the shop once more Susan looked up at Gideon resentfully. 'I'm not sure I quite like being handed around and organised like that. It's very kind of you, of course——' Her voice drifted away as she met his eyes and saw the devilish gleam in them.

'I make a habit of insuring valuable goods,' he said softly. He opened the car door for her and added in a businesslike voice, 'I've arranged to take the car in to the garage to be serviced while I'm away, so I'll have to leave you to get a taxi back. Let's have a quick bite of lunch and then you can come to the airport and see me off.'

It might almost have been a working lunch they had together at a small restaurant near the harbour while Gideon briefed her on details she would need to know in his absence. Susan hardly noticed what she was eating; she couldn't take her eyes off Gideon. I'm crazy, she thought, absolutely crazy, feeling like this about a man I only met a couple of days ago. Two days—two years—what difference did it make? She had once read somewhere that if you're going to fall in love with someone it happens in the first five minutes—though you may not realise it all at once. She had thought that rubbish, but now she knew it was true.

His mind was focussed on more practical matters. 'I think that's all,' he said at last, gulping down a final cup of coffee and consulting his watch. 'I'll ring you each evening just to make sure everything's all right. You'll ring the hospital for news of Ben? The address and telephone number are on the pad. Use Ben's taxi firm for transport and tell them to put it on the bill. Okay?'

After that it was all a mad rush. Gideon dumped his car at the garage, grabbed his briefcase from inside, hailed a taxi and they were at the airport in no time at all.

His flight was called almost as soon as they got inside

the building, and Susan stood back and admired the clipped and efficient way he dealt with the formalities. 'Young man in a hurry,' he grinned at her over his shoulder as they approached the departure point. 'I didn't think I'd cut it quite so fine.'

They stood looking at each other. 'Take care of yourself, little one,' he said, 'and be waiting for me when I get back. We'll dive that wall beyond the lagoon together.' His eyes were glittering in the light filtering through the glass. He put both his arms round her and kissed her lips firmly, almost possessively.

And then he was on his way. Before he passed out of sight he turned and lifted a hand and Susan waved back. This, she thought, was how it would be when he finally walked out of her life for good and it was dust and ashes. Like a little death. Her eyes swimming with tears, she went slowly back to the waiting taxi.

Looking back at them a long time later, the five days that followed seemed the strangest and most contradictory of Susan's whole life. She should have enjoyed every minute of it. She was having the holiday she had always yearned for. Every day she went diving with Mike and one or other of the parties he took out in his boat. She grew to like and admire the tough, red-haired little man. He was a tower of strength to her in her first scuba dive for years. As he helped her into her harness and checked her air tank he grinned cheerily and said, 'I'm going to keep a close eye on you myself this time. Gideon will have my guts for garters if I don't look after you.'

But after one or two dives he was satisfied with her performance and paired her off with one or other in the boat party. Usually it was one of the Fergusons, a family of mother, father and daughter Diane. Diane was a brown-haired girl of fourteen with a brace on her teeth and a good deal of puppy fat that she was just beginning to worry about. She attached herself to Susan right away and followed her everywhere and her parents, obviously relieved to find a responsible, older girl who seemed willing to spend her time with their young daughter, welcomed Susan with enthusiasm.

Like all good Americans on holiday they were keen to see everything there was to be seen, and Susan accompanied them on their outings. They went to the turtle farm that Gideon had pointed out, and exclaimed in amazement at the number of turtles in the different basins — from the tiny hatchlings swimming round briskly in their little circular pools to the huge, elegant breeding turtles in their V.I.P. lagoons with man-made beaches where they could lay their eggs. Diane was fascinated and could only be dragged away by a promise of a present from the gift shop. In the end both she and Susan were presented with a bracelet made from turtle shell.

They explored the island in Mr Ferguson's hired car. One day they drove up to the north coast, through lush countryside with wild orchids, royal palms, and wild parrots, gorgeously coloured, squawking in the branches. They had to visit the post office in Hell again, where Diane sent numerous picture-postcards to her school friends back at home.

The Fergusons were staying at one of the most exclusive hotels on Seven Mile Beach, and here Susan was pressed to join them for dinner each evening. If she had chosen to, she could have spent every hour of the waking day with the happy and companionable family.

But she had other things to consider, and it was those

other things that buzzed like bees at the back of her mind.

Each day she telephoned the hospital in Houston to get a report on Della's Uncle Ben, and it was on the Wednesday—the third day of Gideon's absence—that she got the news that the surgeon in charge of the case had finally decided that an operation would not be necessary. Mr Caldicott would be transferred to the hospital in Grand Cayman in a few days' time, and the treatment would be continued from there.

Later that evening Della telephoned, and Susan told her the news. 'Oh golly, is that good or bad?' Della's clear voice came over the phone from Miami. 'It's good, of course, for Uncle Ben, but how about you, Susan dear? I do feel that Vic and I have been horribly selfish about all this and landed you with all sorts of problems. But if you knew how blissfully happy I am, maybe you'd forgive us and think it's been worthwhile. I'm afraid this Gideon North man's been rather a bore, hasn't he? From your letter he sounds like a right little dictator.'

Susan smiled grimly. 'He thinks I'm you, and he doesn't like rich men's daughters, can you believe it? It was rather edgy at first, but we're on better terms now.' *What* terms? she wondered. She only wished she knew. 'And he's away just at present, so there isn't any problem.'

'Oh, good,' said Della. 'Look, Susan, Vic would like to have a word.'

Vic came on the line next. 'I heard about Della's Uncle Ben coming home,' he said. 'Is it going to put you in a fix—would you like us to come and take over?'

Oh *no*! thought Susan in a panic. That would mean that her job here would be over and she would have to leave and—and she wouldn't see Gideon again. 'That would interfere with your tour, surely?' she said in as calm a voice as she could manage.

'Well, yes, I suppose it would, rather. But if you think——'

'No, really,' Susan put in hastily. 'I'm sure I can cope. I'll write to Mr Caldicott and tell him the whole story, so that he won't get a shock when he arrives and finds me here instead of Della. Then I can see how he takes it, and let you know. How about that?'

They both thought that was a very good idea, and they both overwhelmed Susan with gratitude. They sounded, she thought, as if they had wandered together into the Garden of Eden with never a serpent in sight.

Susan had to remind Vic about the cassette tape and he said he hadn't had time to listen to it yet but he would certainly do so. 'I'll put it on now, we've got a few minutes to spare before the next rehearsal.' He seemed to hesitate. 'Don't hope for too much for this young man, Sue,' he said. 'We get so many of these hopeful song-writers. But I'll certainly hear it.' His voice was warm as he added, 'I'd do more than that for you, Sue—I've so much to thank you for.'

Susan's eyes were soft as she replaced the receiver. It was nice to think that there was one love story that was going to have a happy ending.

She pushed away the telephone and began her letter to Uncle Ben. It took until midnight and she made three attempts before she was finally satisfied that she had explained everything as clearly and truthfully as she could.

She began, 'I meant to tell you the whole truth as soon as I arrived here, and that's what Della wanted too, but I didn't dare to upset you when you were so ill. But now we both want you to know it all.' Then she wrote the whole story, from the moment that John Benton had sacked her from her job, ending with the phone call she had just had from Della and Vic. She put in at the end, 'I haven't been able to tell Mr North the truth, as he mistook me for Della. I didn't know him, and I think you'll understand that I couldn't entrust Della's secret to anybody but you. As you can guess, this has led to a rather awkward situation, but I'm sure it can all be smoothed out when you return. I do hope you're feeling much better. When you get back I'll come to visit you and you can tell me just what you want me to do, and I'll promise to do it. Yours sincerely, Susan French.'

She addressed the letter to the hospital, found stamps in the desk and guessed at the correct ones. Then she went out to the collection box she had seen at the entrance to the condo and slipped the letter in.

When she had done it she felt an enormous weight off her mind. At least somebody—and the most important person—would know the truth now. How Gideon would find it out she didn't dare to think yet.

It was a glorious night, with a nearly-full moon sailing high in the sky, dimming the stars. Susan wandered back, walking on the grass. Writing the letter had exhausted her, and there was something about the beauty of the night that made her want to cry because she didn't know how she was going to get through the next days. Everything was closing in on her now and she thought she knew what it felt like to sit in the dock, waiting for sentence to be passed. And oh, she wanted Gideon here! She longed for him with every nerve and fibre in her body.

There was a movement just ahead and she saw a man coming towards her, a dark form in the shadow of the bushes. For a moment her heart nearly stopped, then she recognised Sebastian.

He greeted her morosely. 'Hullo, Della, I saw you come out.' He turned and walked along beside her. 'I haven't seen you for ages.'

'Three and a half days,' said Susan lightly.

'Feels like three and a half years,' he grumbled. 'It's been hell in there.' He jerked his head towards the apartment. 'Faye's been in a foul mood, dunno why especially. Gideon's away, isn't he, I haven't seen him about lately.'

'Yes, he's away on business.' She didn't want to talk about Gideon, so she went on quickly, 'I've been speaking to Vic on the phone this evening and he's got your cassette tape. He hasn't had time to listen to it yet, but he's promised to, very soon, and he'll get in touch about it.'

'That's terrific!' He cheered up slightly. They had reached the apartment block by now and he began to thank her again. 'You don't know how much it means to me just to have an opinion and——'

'Sorry, Sebastian,' she cut him short, 'I think that's my phone ringing.' She ran in through the open front door and across the sitting room. The hospital? Bad news about Uncle Ben? Oh, please not, she prayed as she lifted the receiver.

It was Gideon. 'Della? You take some waking up, I must say! I've been ringing for the last ten minutes.' He sounded tired and irritable.

'I—I've been out to post a letter.' Her heart was thumping like mad. She sank into a chair beside the desk because her legs wouldn't hold her up. 'H-how are you, Gideon? Are you enjoying your trip?' she babbled nervously.

'Hell, no,' he said. 'It's just one damned meeting on top of another.' Goodness, he *was* in a mood! She waited.

'I've tried to get through to you I don't know how many times, in between meetings and boring late dinners, but every time there's been no reply. What the blazes have you been up to?'

She wasn't going to take that from him. 'I don't think I have to account to you for my movements.' She tried to put some dignity into her voice, but her throat was dry and she merely sounded huffy.

'Oh, for God's sake,' he groaned, 'don't let's start all that again!'

There was a long pause and she began to think he had rung off. Then he said in a milder tone, 'I only wanted to make sure that things were going all right at your end.'

'Oh yes,' she said brightly. 'I'm having a super time. Mike's been wonderful, taking me out in the boat with him, and I've met a lot of nice people and the diving's been absolutely fantastic. I was taken out to dinner last night at the Holiday Inn and——'

'Good,' he interrupted. 'Good. You needn't give me the full catalogue of your amusements. I'm glad you're having a good time.' He didn't sound at all glad.

'Do you—can you say when you'll be back?' Susan tried not to sound too eager.

'Friday, definitely. Expect me some time late afternoon.'

Her spirits lifted. Only two more days—one and a half really. She said, 'I've been in touch with the hospital in Houston each day. They say that they may transfer Uncle Ben to the hospital here quite soon.'

'Yes, I know. He'll be glad to be back nearer home.'

There was another long pause and then Gideon said in an odd, jerky way, 'Are you missing me at all, Della?'

The room swam before her eyes. 'I—I——' she gulped. 'Yes, of course I am,' she managed to get out. 'But I'm not here very much,' she added, and then wished she hadn't.

'No, obviously not,' said Gideon. 'Goodbye then, Della. Enjoy yourself. I'll ring again if I have an opportunity.'

'Yes, do,' she said. 'Goodbye, Gideon.'

She fumbled the receiver back on to its cradle and sat staring at it despondently. What a horrid, unsatisfactory thing a telephone could be!

She crawled upstairs to bed, but it was a long time before she fell asleep.

Mike was working the air-compressor unit when Susan arrived at his dive shop next morning. He stopped when he saw her come in and greeted her cheerily.

She came over to his work-bench. 'Mike, will it put you out if I don't come in the boat with you this afternoon?'

He smiled his slow smile. 'That's a coincidence. The Fergusons have cancelled too. Mr F.'s had an urgent recall from his firm and they're rushing back home to Pittsburg. They called in to pick up their gear not an hour ago. Young Diane was in quite a state about not being able to see you to say goodbye. She asked me to give you this.' He handed Susan a folded note that had been propped up on his work-bench.

Susan unfolded it. 'Darling Susan,' Diane had written in a careful sloping hand, 'We've got to go back home today, isn't it just awful? I guess I could sock those people in Pop's office. It's been great knowing you and I'll miss you so much. Will you be in the Caymans when we come back next year? Will you write to me? I've put my address underneath. I've got to rush now, Mom's screaming at me. Weren't our dives wonderful? With love from Diane.'

Susan smiled and put the note in her bag. She'd certainly write to Diane, but just as certainly she wouldn't see her next year in the Caymans.

Mike said, 'Heard when Gideon's coming back yet?'

'Yes, tomorrow. That's why I'm going to be busy—shopping in food and so on.' She had a plan for Gideon's return. He would probably be hungry and certainly he would be tired. She would have a meal ready for him at the condo and they would eat together, just the two of them, looking out at the sunset——

Mike nodded, his leathery face creased thoughtfully. 'He's a good chap, Gideon, one of the best. Had a rough time of it lately.' He glanced briefly at her and then away again. 'Has he told you about his parents?'

'No. I—I've only known him a few days.'

'Is that so?' said Mike, surprised. 'I'd have thought——' He looked faintly embarrassed.

Susan asked, 'What about his parents?'

Mike shook his head. 'A tragedy, one of the real tragedies. Wonderful people, both of them, I'd known them for years. We did a lot of diving together. I was a pro and they were amateurs, of course, but they knew all there was to know about it. Used to spend all their holidays on projects, and they brought Gideon up to go along with them. It was last summer it happened, somewhere over in Scotland—they were working on a wartime wreck.' He shrugged. 'It was never found out exactly what did happen.'

'They were both—drowned?' Susan had gone cold all over.

Mike nodded. 'Of course, they were getting on a bit, but that wasn't it—couldn't have been. They were both as fit as fiddles—they were over here visiting Gideon only the week before and I was diving with the three of them myself. No,' he said slowly, 'there's always the risk in this game.'

The sunny day seemed darker when Susan went out. She went into a coffee shop near the harbour and drank strong black coffee. She had a strange feeling of grief for two people she had never known, and she understood so much more now about their son. Understood why he had seemed so dictatorial and unreasonable about her wanting to dive. Understood, too, a little about his swings of mood. You didn't get over a shock like that for a long time, as she knew only too well. Her heart melted for him, but she wouldn't be able to show it, she thought wryly. Instead, she would see that he had a good meal when he got home tomorrow. She could at least do that for him.

She finished her coffee and went out to look for a shopping centre where she could buy in food. In an odd way she felt happier than she had done since she arrived here. She kept on hearing the way he had said, 'Are you missing me at all, Della?' and suddenly she felt close to him.

For the very first time she allowed herself to hope.

CHAPTER EIGHT

THE taxi driver unloaded Susan's various bags of provisions and smilingly tucked his tip into the pocket of his jeans. 'Carry 'em up for you, missus?' His grin was nearly as broad as the brim of his straw hat.

'No need, I'll do that,' said a voice from behind.

Susan spun round to see a tall young man with floppy hair walking towards her across the patio. She stared for a moment. Then, 'Vic!' she cried, and ran to meet him.

He hugged her as if she were a long-lost sister and she hugged him back. 'What a lovely surprise!' She glanced around. 'Is Della with you?'

'No.' Vic picked up the bags, shaking his head regretfully. 'We thought it mightn't be quite safe yet for her to appear.'

She led him into the sitting room and pushed him into a chair while she fussed round, pouring out drinks. 'What's happened? Why are you here? Nothing's wrong, is it?'

'Golly, no,' said Vic. 'Everything's gloriously right. We're off to Mexico tomorrow after a couple of encouraging shows in Miami. And——' he stopped '—there's nobody else here, is there?'

'No—go on.'

'And we're going to be married in Mexico City as soon as we can,' he announced triumphantly. 'Della's taken to the crazy life like a good trouper. She's the craziest of the lot of us.'

'Oh, Vic, I'm so glad! It's made everything worth-while.' Susan raised her glass of pineapple juice. 'Here's to both of you.'

'Thanks, Sue, I knew you'd be glad. I really wanted to hop over here and see you and thank you for all you've done before we finally disappear into the far distance. We thought we'd hide in Mexico City—it's big enough, goodness knows—until the knot is tied. After that, thank God, we won't need to hide. We'll go back and tell Della's awful father. I want to see his face.'

'It won't be very pretty,' said Susan.

'It's got to be done, though. Della's got to face him some time, and I'll be there with her, he'll have me to reckon with. But you know, Sue,' he went on seriously, 'Della's changing. She's gaining confidence every day she's away from her father. She's superb.' His face went dreamy. 'She's just one of us, and the boys absolutely worship her.'

Susan twiddled the stem of her glass in her hand. 'Do you think, then, I could tell Gideon—Mr North—the truth now? Explain everything to him? It's been a bit awkward, pretending to be Della, but it seemed the only thing to do, as Uncle Ben wasn't here.'

'You've carried it all off wonderfully, and this North man sounds rather a pain in the neck, so I'm sure it hasn't been easy for you. Yes, tell him now, why not? It'll make things easier for you while you're here, and it can hardly get back to Della's father in time to spoil our plans. He'd never find us in Mexico City—eight million inhabitants, isn't it? Or is it ten million?' He grinned complacently. 'Miami has been rather a cliff-hanger. We made quite a hit there and the local papers have been having a ball, with photographs and so on, but in Mexico we'll be anonymous.' He grinned again, his eyes twinkling. 'At least until we've given one or two shows, then we'll be top-line raves. I hope!'

Vic crossed his fingers and waved them in the air, but just for a second Susan saw fear cross his face—the fear that attacks all artists who have to face the public and put themselves to the test. She liked and admired him even more.

'But let's stop talking about me,' he said. 'How is Della's Uncle Ben getting along? She said to be sure to ask you.'

She told him the latest news from the hospital. 'It looks as if he may be coming home in a few days. I wrote to him yesterday, explaining everything, so the ground is prepared for when he arrives—if I'm still here. Do you—do you want me to stay on any longer?' Oh, please say yes. Please, please say yes! Give me time to tell Gideon the truth in my own way, so that he won't feel badly about everything.

'If you can bear it,' said Vic, 'we thought if you'd just stay until we're well and truly spliced. We'll let you know the moment and then, of course, you can make your way back to England any time. I wish you could come to the wedding. Della's busy shopping this afternoon—buying a super new outfit——'

His eyes had gone dreamy again. He would have gone on talking about Della indefinitely if Susan hadn't stopped him to ask if he was travelling back this evening.

He shook his head. 'Couldn't get a flight until tomorrow morning. I've booked in for the night at a hotel just along from here. Also—oh, gosh, I nearly forgot—I wondered if I could meet this bloke who made the tape you sent me. Is he around?'

'Sebastian Lord? He's living in the next apartment with his sister. What did you think—was his music any good?'

'Might be. Might well be. It wants knocking into shape, but we all think he may be what we're looking for. I'd like to talk to him—maybe hear some more of his stuff. I wonder if he's at home?'

Susan wasn't going to knock on Faye Lord's door if she could help it, but Vic had no such inhibitions. He went out and was back a few minutes later, with Sebastian trailing behind him—his guitar under his arm and a bemused expression on his sad clown's face.

It was a long evening. Once Vic and Sebastian got talking music Susan left them to it. She made heaps of sandwiches and chilled plenty of cans of beer, and then she sat back in a corner trying to look interested until she realised that they were living in a world of their own and weren't really aware of her existence. Finally, when she couldn't hold her eyelids open any longer, she said goodnight and went up to bed, hugging to herself the knowledge that tomorrow she would see Gideon again. The last thing she heard was the soft strumming of Sebastian's guitar in the room below.

She was just in the process of waking up next morning when Adèle came into the bedroom. Her eyes were round, her white smile gleaming wickedly. 'Miss, do you know about the man who's asleep downstairs? I just saw the back of 'is 'ead in the armchair, but I didn't wake 'im up.'

Susan sat up. 'Man?' she squeaked. She dragged on a wrap and followed Adèle downstairs. It couldn't be Gideon? He couldn't have come home late and——

It was Vic, of course. He was just waking up when they went in, blinking against the sunlight pouring through the big window. 'Gosh!' He looked round him dazedly and then at Susan. 'I must have dropped off— we kept it up rather late. When Seb left I thought I'd just have another drink. I must have gone out like a light.'

He didn't look like a man with a hangover. It had been sheer fatigue, Susan guessed, not the beer.

He looked at his watch, pushing back his flop of hair. 'Cripes, I'm going to miss my flight if I don't get a move on. I've got to get to the hotel and pick up my bag. It's only a couple of minutes from here, I can walk, then I can get a taxi to the airport from there.' He stood up and fingered his chin. 'Do I look a wreck? Oh well——'

Susan went out on to the patio with him. 'Goodbye, Vic, love to Della, and all the very best to you both.'

'Thanks, Sue, we love you.' He put his arms round her and kissed her and then raced away along the service road.

Susan stood considering the day ahead; she would plan it carefully so nothing would spoil Gideon's homecoming. She had no idea when he would arrive, but he'd said 'Friday, for sure.' Probably some time late afternoon or early evening. She had heard that there was a complicated network of air-routes linking up the Caribbean Islands, but there was no way of finding out how he would get here from Tobago. She would just have to wait.

The waiting was going to be agony and the day stretched ahead endlessly. She would have to try to keep busy. She put on a bikini and swam up and down the empty swimming pool as if she were training for the Olympics, keeping an eye on the place where Gideon's car would appear round the bushes—just as if he could possibly get here this early.

Back in the apartment she showered and washed her hair and sat out on the balcony of her bedroom to brush-dry it. Adèle came up with coffee and rolls on a tray. Susan drank the coffee, but the rolls stuck in her throat however much butter she plastered on them.

The sun was hotter now and she still had to take care about getting burned. She went back into the bedroom, stripped off, and examined herself in the long mirror. Not exactly a sun-tan, perhaps, but her skin looked good—creamy and smooth. For some reason she blushed and turned to the clothes cupboard.

Not a top and jeans today; something more—more feminine. She chose a little cotton number, white and lime green with ruched shoulder straps and a tiny frill round the hem. Then she went downstairs to ask Adèle's advice about preparing some side-dishes to serve with the impressive dressed lobster sitting waiting in the fridge.

Adèle was delighted at being consulted. 'Mr North, 'e come back today and you having everything nice for him, eh?' Her black eyes sparkled mischievously and Susan felt herself blush again. This was terrible!

'He'll be tired and need a good meal,' she said, sounding as practical and offhand as she could.

Adèle was a tower of strength. She had all sorts of ideas about doing clever things with pigeon peas, tiny onions and tomatoes, carrots and asparagus, rice, basted with olive oil and pepped up with spices. There was the inevitable avocado; and peaches soaked in Bacardi with coconut cream. There was the long French loaf that Adèle had brought with her from her father's bakery at the restaurant, and white wine that could be chilled later.

Adèle surveyed her handiwork with approval. 'My father, 'e should be cross that you do not eat at the restaurant, but I think he understand that sometimes there must be a tête-à tête, yes?'

At ten o'clock Adèle left and Susan made herself some more coffee and managed to swallow a couple of biscuits.

By eleven she had checked everything in the fridge three times and found a pretty flower-trimmed cloth to spread on the table, polished the cutlery and been out to pick some tiny star-shaped blue flowers whose name she didn't know, to arrange in a white pottery jug she had found in the kitchen.

At half-past eleven Sebastian called in. He wasn't looking like a sad clown any longer. He was beaming like a lighthouse. 'Can't stop,' he said. 'I'm working on a new song. Just had to come in to thank you for everything, Della. Vic's a great chap, isn't he? He seemed quite interested in my stuff—he asked me to go out to Mexico next week and meet the rest of his group. How's that, then?' He grabbed Susan round the waist and whirled her gleefully.

'Stop!' she gasped. She was quite sufficiently worked up as it was, without having any more adrenalin pumping round her.

He let her go and she flopped into a chair. Sebastian stood over her, waving his arms, his striped shirt flapping. 'Free at last!' he carolled. 'My luck's turned, for sure. Faye's leaving this afternoon. She's given up Gideon and got an oil-man in tow. She's wangled an invite for herself to some place in Texas and she's off this afternoon.'

It was lovely to see him so happy. Susan was glad for him and said so.

'You brought me luck, sweetheart.' He leaned down and kissed her heartily. 'It's all your doing.'

She sat smiling when he'd gone. Little Miss Fix-it, that's me, she thought. Everyone loves me—Vic, Della,

Sebastian. She crossed her fingers. And Gideon? Her stomach lurched uneasily. She would have to wait to find that out.

The time crawled by. Everything was prepared, there was nothing left to do. She wandered round the apartment, first hot and then cold, as she tried to think up ways of beginning to tell him. She rushed to the window every time a car passed along the service road or pulled up outside. She read two articles in a geographical magazine and didn't take in a word of them. By three o'clock she was almost a nervous wreck.

And then he came. She heard the car first and he came striding into the room before she had time to pull herself together. He looked tired but he looked wonderful. Her eyes drank in every bit of him—the lean body, the thin, strong face, the piercing grey eyes with their curtain of curving black lashes, the way his hair grew thick round his ears.

She came towards him. 'Hullo,' she said, and—foolishly—'You're back.'

Gideon stood still, just looking at her. 'I've got some food ready,' she gabbled. 'A late lunch or a high tea or whatever. I—I thought you might like to eat here if you're tired after travelling.'

He looked at the table set with its flowery cloth, its shining silver, its little white bowl of flowers. 'It feels like home,' he said. He smiled at her and her heart turned over.

'Did you have a good trip? A good journey?' The words seemed to come from somewhere above her head. She felt as if she were floating inches off the ground.

'A satisfactory trip,' she said. 'Tobago is a pleasant place, but I didn't notice very much of it.' He put his hand in his pocket and pulled out a small parcel. 'I brought you a memento.'

'Oh!' she gasped, the colour flooding into her face. She fumbled with the wrapping and at last uncovered a leather box that snapped open to disclose a necklace lying on the folds of white satin—a thin twisted rope of silver and gold. She lifted startled eyes to Gideon's. 'It's—it's absolutely wonderful! But you shouldn't have bought me something like this—it must have cost the earth!' It never occurred to her that John Benton's daughter would not be over-impressed by an expensive present. 'Oh, it's beautiful.' She went across to the wall mirror and held the chain against her neck. 'Thank you, Gideon.'

He took it trom her and unfastened the clasp. 'It goes on like this,' he said. 'Yes,' he lifted the chain gently and let it fall back against the creamy flesh of her neck, '—I pictured it looking just like that.'

Their eyes met in the mirror for a long moment and Susan felt as if she were suffocating. 'You must be hungry,' she said in a high, tight voice. 'Would you like to shower and change while I put the food on the table?'

His hands were resting on her shoulders. 'There's something else I should like first,' he said softly, turning her round.

His eyes roamed over her face as if he were seeing her for the first time. 'I've missed you, Della,' he said. 'I've missed you like hell.'

Her eyes pricked with tears. If only he hadn't called her Della! But this wasn't the moment for explanations. 'I've missed you too,' she murmured unsteadily.

He drew her into his arms, holding her tightly against his body with a kind of hunger. 'It's the devil, starting something you don't finish,' he muttered thickly.

She could feel his heart beating strongly against her

and joy was flowering inside her, opening like the petals of the great poinciana blossoms hanging outside the window.

From a great distance she was aware of a bell ringing. 'Go away,' muttered Gideon against her ear. 'Go away, blast you!'

It rang again. Then a feminine voice came from the direction of the window. 'May I come in?' said Faye Lord. '*So* sorry to disturb your homecoming, Gideon.' She wore a clinging outfit, and her voice was silky. 'I *did* ring the bell, but you were—er—too occupied to hear it.' She came farther into the room, her smile not reaching her green, narrowed eyes. 'I just had to drop in to say goodbye,' she said. 'I'm off to visit some friends in Dallas. Sebastian is driving me to the airport. I doubt if I'll be coming back to the Caymans, so this is really goodbye.' She put a hand on Gideon's arm and reached up and kissed his cheek. 'It's been nice knowing you, Gideon, we've had fun, haven't we?'

She didn't seem to notice that he didn't reply. She turned to Susan, who had moved away to stand beside the desk. 'Goodbye, Della, and the best of luck.' The green eyes narrowed still further and the smile became feline. 'Did you have a good time last night? I saw you bidding a fond farewell to your boy-friend early this morning.' Her laugh was metallic. 'You should really be more careful where you indulge in smooching at that time in the morning. It puts ideas in people's heads.'

An impatient peep-peep sounded from outside. 'Heavens, I must dash or I'll miss my flight!' Faye lifted a fluttering hand. 'Bless you, my children,' she cried gaily, and ran across the patio to the waiting car.

Silence closed over the room. Gideon stood very still and his face was white under its tan. 'Well,' he said quietly, 'Is it true?'

'Is—is what true?' Susan stalled. She hardly knew what she was saying. The expression on his face terrified her.

He took a step towards her and she shrank back against the desk, the edge pressing into her thighs painfully.

'You know bloody well what I mean. Was it this fellow Vic who was here last night, and did he stay here and leave this morning?'

She lifted her head high. 'Yes, Vic was here, but——'

'Well then,' he said, and she had never heard anything as cold as his voice, 'that seems to cover everything, doesn't it?'

'Gideon—please—it's not what you think. I——'

'I don't *think*, I know.' His lip curled. 'I ought to have known before. I was right about you from the beginning—you and your precious father. Vic was someone you had to play down, wasn't he, until you had me eating out of your hand. Then as soon as I was out of the way he comes crawling into my home and no doubt into your bed. What a bloody fool I was to think——'

Tears welled into her eyes and slid down her cheeks. 'Stop—stop——' she sobbed. 'You've got it all wrong—everything. It's not like that at all. *Will* you just listen for a minute—I can explain——'

He had turned away and she grasped his arm, but he shook off her hand. 'I bet you can explain.' He bit out the words. 'I'm sure you're very good at explaining, but I don't think I want to listen.' He picked up his briefcase and strode out of the room.

Susan stumbled upstairs and closed her bedroom door as if she could somehow shut out the ugliness of what had happened. She sat on the bed, shivering. But after a moment she stopped crying and went over to the washbasin to mop her eyes. It was no good letting herself go to bits. Gideon would come back, he would have to come back, and then he would be in a more reasonable mood and she would *make* him listen to her.

She heard a car door slam; he had gone. But then there was the sound of men's voices, Gideon's and another one. They came nearer. They rumbled on inside the house now, in the room below. There was a short silence, then,

'Della—are you up there?' It was Gideon calling, brusquely.

She didn't move or reply; she couldn't go down in this state, not if he had someone with him. Who could it be? Sebastian? Mike, perhaps?

'Della!' he called again. 'You'd better come down. Your father is here.'

When disaster strikes there is a period of numbness when you feel nothing. Susan had reached it. After a moment or two she got up and walked down the stairs stiffly; her legs felt like a puppet's legs, her eyes were blank.

John Benton was standing with his back to the table, his thinning hair clinging damply to his red face, his mouth shut like a trap. He held a folded newspaper in front of him.

He glanced only briefly at her out of bloodshot eyes. 'So you're here, are you? Well, perhaps you'll tell me the meaning of this——' He held the newspaper up and slapped it viciously several times. She saw a photograph of two people coming out of a building and the caption below in bold letters: *Singing star Vic Wild and his Bride-to-Be*.

She stood like a statue while John Benton came across the room towards her. The way his face changed had something comically horrible about it. 'My God,' he spluttered. 'You! What the hell are you doing here? Where's Della? Where's my daughter?'

She felt quite calm. She said, 'I don't know. But I don't think you'll find her in a hurry, wherever she is.'

He exploded then. 'You little tramp, you've been passing yourself off as Della! Where is she—what's happened to her—what does this mean?' He thrust the paper before her eyes, his purplish face only inches from hers, his head lowered like an angry bull.

Susan was afraid he would have a stroke at any moment. 'I told you, I don't know where she is, but it's no good you looking for her. She'll be married before you find her—I *do* know that.'

The man was shaking, out of control. 'You bitch— you dirty little cheat——' His language became more violent as the filthy words poured out. 'I might have known you were up to something—that you'd try to spite me! I could——'

He lifted a heavy arm to strike her and she shrank back against the doorpost, but Gideon was there in front of her.

'I think you'd better leave, Mr Benton,' he said, and after the angry heat of the other man's bellowings his voice cut through the room like a cold steel blade. 'This lady is staying in my house and is under my protection.'

John Benton glared at him. 'You're in this too, are you? Get out of my way, you——'

Gideon's hands closed on the flailing arms. For a moment Susan thought there was going to be a fight, but Gideon's strength had the older man writhing helplessly. His hands were pinioned behind his back and he was being propelled through the front door, still threatening and cursing.

The sound of a car engine died away in the distance. After what seemed like hours Gideon came in and stood in the hall, wiping his hands on a clean white handkerchief as if they had been contaminated.

He looked at Susan, his face expressionless. 'So,' he said, 'it turned out to be an even more complicated web of deceit than it seemed.'

The urge to explain, to make him listen, had left her now. Something in his face had killed it. She said dully, 'If you would listen, I could tell you everything—the whole story.'

He smiled thinly. 'I'm sure you could. But what makes you think I would believe you?' She made a helpless little gesture and he went on, 'There's only one question I'd like answered. You're not, I take it, Della Benton?'

'No,' she said tonelessly.

'That's all I want to know.'

She swallowed with difficulty. 'It would be—kind of you to listen. It would be fair.'

'Fair?' You've hardly been fair to me. You've been lying to me and putting on an act ever since you arrived. Was that fair? Why should I be fair to you now?'

Only if you loved me, she thought. If you loved me you would be angry, hurt, bewildered. There wouldn't be this terrible bleakness, this high wall between us.

She said, 'I'd like to leave here as soon as possible. I have my return ticket to London.'

'Very good idea.' He walked past her into the sitting room and picked up the phone. 'I'll see what I can arrange.'

Susan stood stiffly, her hands locked on the door-frame behind her, hearing his voice but not listening.

When he replaced the receiver he said, 'They have a seat on an extra flight to Miami in just under an hour. I suggest you pack as quickly as you can and I'll take you to the airport.'

'Couldn't I get a taxi?' she said faintly.

'I prefer to take you myself.' Of course—to make sure she went. To see her off the premises like a criminal.

Upstairs in her bedroom she changed into the travelling suit she had worn when she arrived and threw a few of her personal possessions into a small bag she could take as hand luggage. She couldn't cope with the hassle of anything heavier or bulkier. She slid the wardrobe door closed on all the pretty dresses inside. Della could claim them in due course.

Susan swilled her face, smoothed her hair and leaned to the mirror to outline her mouth defiantly with rosered lipstick. There was nothing she could do about her face. She was in a state of shock, and she looked it.

She walked stiffly downstairs. 'I'm ready,' she said. She felt like a French aristocrat climbing into the tumbril on the way to the guillotine. She had to bite her lip hard to stop herself bursting into hysterical laughter.

Not a word was exchanged on the drive to the airport. Here, Gideon carried her bag to the departures desk and put it down beside her.

He spoke then. He said, 'You'll have to arrange your own link-up flight when you get to Miami.'

'Yes,' she said, 'I'll do that.' She bent her head over her handbag, groping inside for her papers. 'Goodbye, Gideon,' she said.

She didn't raise her head. If she had seen his face again she would have burst into tears.

She thought he said, 'Goodbye,' but she couldn't be

sure. When she allowed herself to look up again he had gone.

CHAPTER NINE

It wasn't until Susan was actually back in London, some thirty-six hours later, that she realised that Christmas was only days away. Through the misty windows of the bus that brought her from the airport she saw shop windows glittering in the dusk; fairy-lights garlanding the streets, shopping crowds surging along the pavements. It was damp and cold, but the feel of Christmas hung over everything. Turkey and holly and the smell of pine needles and Christmas pudding. New toys and laughter and tears. Everything the cynics professed to despise. Including love, she thought bleakly. Most of all, love.

At the hostel she found Mrs Benson, the caretaker, hanging up pink and blue paper-chains in the common room. Serinder, the Indian student, was holding the ladder for her.

Mrs Benson was a friendly soul. 'Hullo, ducks, you back?' she greeted Susan. 'Had a lovely holiday? Bet it was warmer there than here.'

Susan put on a bright smile. 'Yes, thank you, Mrs Benson, I had a very good time.'

'You haven't got yourself much of a sun-tan.' The caretaker steadied herself against the picture-rail, peering down.

'I wasn't there long enough. You have to take care not to get burned.' (Gideon's voice saying, 'You don't know you're getting burned until it's too late.' Oh God, she thought hopelessly.)

Mrs Benson climbed down the ladder. 'You'll be here for the Christmas Eve party, then? We're going to have quite a do this year. There'll be six of the girls staying on and they're all bringing their boy-friends. Gillian's David is going to fix up a hi-fi for us. And it'll be a celebration, too. Serinder has passed her exams—she's a real doctor now.'

Serinder's beautiful serene face broke into a smile as Susan congratulated her. She moved her hips and her sari swung gracefully. 'I am to be married soon and then we will go back to India together to help our own people.' Pride and happiness shone from her great dark eyes.

Susan knew she couldn't take the party. 'I'm afraid I shan't be here for Christmas, Mrs Benson. I'm going down to Devon, I have friends there.' Some of her old school friends might still be around, if they weren't all married. It was sad how soon you lost touch, once you moved away.

'Whereabouts?' enquired Mrs Benson chattily. 'Joe and me went to Torquay for our honeymoon.' She sighed gustily, and blew her nose hard. 'Happy days!'

'Oh, not as far as Torquay. And not as expensive either!' Susan said. 'Breaton. Just a little place on the coast that hardly anybody's heard of.' It was true; if you wanted to disappear what better place than Breaton? And just now she wanted, more than anything else, to disappear, to go to ground in the place where she had been happy. Just for a while. Just until she had got Gideon North out of her system and didn't feel like bursting into stupid tears whenever she had to talk to anybody.

Getting to Breaton on Christmas Eve wasn't easy. Fast train—slow train—bus. Finding somewhere to sleep wasn't easy either. Breaton was probably the tiniest of holiday resorts along the coast. It put up its shutters to visitors at the end of September and kept them closed until May.

But the landlady of the Barley Sheaf remembered Susan from the days when her father had brought her here after their diving expeditions and she had sat outside on a bench drinking lemonade while he had his two half-pints of beer at the bar.

'I suppose I could do you bed and breakfast if you like, m'dear,' she offered, rather reluctantly. 'You'll be having your Christmas dinner with friends, you said?'

Susan hadn't said, but she nodded vaguely. Christmas dinner was something she wanted to avoid. So she bought in some cheese and apples and biscuits at the little village shop, and a couple of cans of Coke at the bar of the pub. That would see her through until breakfast on Boxing Day.

Her little room was over the bar and the locals kept it up late on Christmas Eve, but at last the singing stopped and Susan slept, through sheer exhaustion.

Christmas Day was overcast—no rain but no hint of sun either. After making herself eat all the bacon and sausage that the landlady served up to her in the little, chilly parlour, Susan pulled her windcheater over her jeans and woolly sweater and set out. She was going on a sentimental journey—back to the cottage where she had been happy. She had a vague idea that just seeing it might give her a feeling of peace and soften the hard lump of misery that had settled inside her when Gideon walked away from her at the airport in Grand Cayman.

It was a two-mile walk along steep, high-banked lanes and over heathland. The trees dripped with moisture as she went.

The cottage was a disappointment. Everything was changed. The garden had been dug up and neat rows of cabbages and brussels sprouts stood like soldiers where there had once been a riot of flowers. A wrought-iron gate had replaced the old wooden one that she had swung on, and the apple tree she had climbed had been cut down. Worst of all, the roof was no longer thatched, but covered in neat red tiles.

Susan stood at a little distance from the gate, looking up the path, and a small, aggressive mongrel dog advanced and snarled at her, baring its sharp little teeth.

'It only needed you,' she said to it, and turned away.

She had been foolish to come. Nostalgia was a dangerous and uncertain drug. As soon as the trains were running again she would go back to London and pick up the threads of her life. Do the thing she had been trained for; work her way up again.

Men? Well, she would take that as it came. There were other men in the world besides Gideon North, weren't there? *Weren't there?* It had just been a brief encounter and the pain she was feeling all the time would go away eventually. One day, she told herself, as she walked along the silent, dripping lanes, she wouldn't see that thin, hard face every time she closed her eyes, or hear that deep, mocking voice say, 'It's the devil, starting something you don't finish.' That had been all he had wanted of her.

Back in Breaton the mist was really closing down. The red cliffs had disappeared entirely and swirls of white dampness clung to her face and hair as she made her way along the promenade, back towards the Barley Sheaf. She wondered if their Christmas dinner was over by now and how soon she could reasonably go back to her room and eat her apple and cheese. Perhaps she could steal in by a side door while the bar was closed and the family was celebrating.

It was eerie, walking along the deserted promenade with the mist blanketing everything more than a few yards away. Susan could just see the strip of wet sand below and the edge of the tide, as thin waves broke silently over each other in long, sluggish lines. The bathing huts tucked into the promenade wall would be repainted by May, but now they were dull and shabby, their paint peeling, their padlocks hanging on rusty chains.

The silence was somehow frightening. The thick soles of Susan's walking shoes made no sound. Even the sea-gulls were muted as they swooped and settled. Then, out to sea, a fog-siren wailed and she jumped nervously, her heart thumping.

'Stupid,' she said aloud, and quickened her pace.

She knew this little promenade so well; she even knew where she was by counting the shelters. She was nearly at the last one when she saw a large, dark figure looming out of the mist towards her.

She stood still, her mouth suddenly dry, her scalp pricking. Fight or flight, she thought wildly, but she couldn't move.

The figure got nearer, huge and menacing. Her blood froze. It was upon her now, towering above her. As it stopped she gave a gasp of sheer terror.

'I thought I might find you out here,' said Gideon.

Her knees buckled and she slid into his arms.

When she opened her eyes she was lying flat on her back on the slatted wooden seat of the shelter and Gideon was kneeling beside her, stroking her hair back from her forehead.

'It *is* you,' She started to giggle weakly. 'I thought

you were a spook, coming out of the mist at me.' She started to struggle up, but he pushed her back gently.

'Lie still, my darling,' he said. 'I'll go and get my car. Just give me three minutes.'

He was back again in two, a car panting somewhere behind him. He lifted her in his arms and carried her to where it stood, the door swinging open.

The car was warm and roomy. Susan lay in the front seat and closed her eyes. In a few minutes the Barley Sheaf emerged from the mist, its windows alight. Gideon looked at her and said, 'Do you feel up to coming in and packing your things?'

She nodded and he came round and helped her out of the car. Then he thumped on the front door. After an interval it opened and the landlady's head appeared, wearing a red paper hat with a green tassel. 'You found her, then?' she said.

'Yes, I found her.' Gideon had his foot on the step. 'May we come in?'

The landlady beamed on him. 'We're having a bit of a party—you're welcome to join us if you like, m'dears.'

'Thank you very much, but we've got a long drive ahead of us,' Gideon told her.

She nodded at them both and smiled knowingly. 'Enjoy yourselves, then,' she said. 'And a happy Christmas. Close the door when you go, will you?'

Gideon followed Susan up the narrow staircase and stood in the doorway while she packed the few things she had brought with her. Thank goodness, she thought, she had put in a pretty dress at the last moment. She didn't know where they were going, but wherever it was pants and a windcheater didn't seem very appropriate.

When she had closed the case Gideon came across

and put both his hands on her shoulders, looking deeply into her eyes as the sounds of the party drifted up to them from below.

He said, 'I've come half-way across the world to ask you to forgive me, my love. Will you?'

She looked back at him, with the mist glistening on his hair, and his brow furrowed with uncertainty, and a blaze of love in his eyes.

'Yes,' she said. 'Oh yes,' and heard him let out his breath on a sigh.

He drew her into his arms and kissed her lips hard and long. When he lifted his head he was smiling. 'That will have to do for the moment,' he said. He picked up her case and led the way downstairs. As she followed Susan felt as if she were floating three inches off the ground.

At the door she paused. 'I haven't paid my bill.'

'Don't worry, I've settled up for you already. Mine hostess seemed quite satisfied.'

'You were sure I'd come with you?' She tried to sound indignant.

'If you'd refused I'd have sat in the cold on the step until you gave in,' he grinned. He closed the front door on the sound of the party and the amplified boom of an old Val Doonican song was shut off abruptly.

They had left the maze of steep, dripping narrow lanes behind and were clear away from the sea-mist and out on the main road before Gideon spoke again. He said, 'We'll make for Winchester and get on the motor-way. It'll be quicker like that.'

Only then did Susan rouse herself from the warm, hazy stupor she had fallen in to say, 'Where are we going?'

'London. I've got the loan of a friend's flat. He's

away for Christmas.' He flicked a glance towards her. 'It's a very comfortable flat.'

'I'm sure it is,' she said in a polite little voice. She wouldn't have cared if it were a dog kennel, so long as they were together, but Gideon had some explaining to do before she admitted that.

Before they joined the motorway Gideon pulled the car into a layby and switched off the engine and the headlights. It was quite dark now, under the overhanging trees. 'This is a hired car,' he said. 'I don't want to push her too hard. It would be too bad to end Christmas Day waiting for the motorway patrol to tow us away.'

He leaned his head back against the headrest in silence for a time. Then he began to talk quite naturally and evenly, almost as if he were telling her a story.

He said, 'When I got back to the apartment that day I knew I'd made the most awful blunder of my whole life. Me and my bloody stiff-necked pride! You'd gone and I didn't know where. You'd wanted to explain and I wouldn't listen. God, I think I went a bit crazy. I didn't even know your name—that was incredible. I scoured the apartment for some clue and found absolutely nothing. Nothing but the dresses you'd worn. They hit me pretty hard. Then I found that you'd left behind that little bauble I brought you from Tobago, and that hit even harder. I went downstairs and got rather drunk. That didn't help much. I tried Sebastian, but I didn't get much sense out of him except that this bloke called Vic had come over there to interview him about some song-writing or something. To interview *him*! That gave me a glimmer of hope for the first time, but I still couldn't see any daylight. Next morning I pulled myself together and really began to think. I got on the first plane to Houston and went to see Ben at the hospital. He showed me your letter, bless him, and after that everything was clear. But I wasn't any nearer finding you.'

He drew in a deep breath and let it out again. Susan sat staring ahead through the windscreen to where the sidelights made patches of white on the leafless hedge.

He went on, 'I had to wait for two whole days until Della——' he turned his head and in the dim light she saw his smile '—the real Della, I mean—phoned to say that she and her Vic had got married. After a few explanations I found that they had the address of your hostel in London. I packed my bag and put the fear of God in my travel agent, and was in London in twelve hours, even allowing for the time lapse. I parked my bag with Charles at his flat and fixed things up, then I took my courage in both hands and drove to your hostel. There I lost the trail again. The caretaker said you'd gone to spend Christmas at some little place on the coast in Devon, she couldn't remember the name. Somewhere this side of Torquay—Leaton, she thought, or Cleaton, or something. A map gave me Seaton and Breaton and I tossed up, and went to hire a car. My luck turned then. I was going to knock on every door in Breaton until I found you. I tried the only pub in the place first and—you know the rest.'

He turned to her. 'That's my story,' he said. 'I'm in your hands now, Susan. Susan——' he lingered over the name '—it suits you better than Della.' His voice shook a little. 'I'm fathoms deep in love with you, my darling. I think I was from the very beginning, but I had my life all planned out, I believed, and the girl you seemed to be didn't fit into it. I thought I was immune, but you crept into my heart and stayed there.' He drew in a breath. 'Would you consider marrying me?'

Her voice wouldn't work, but she must have swayed towards him because the next moment his arms were holding her as if he would never let her go and his face was buried in her neck.

'My love——' he groaned as he took her lips in a long, possessive kiss. His hand found its way under her soft, woolly sweater and closed over the lacy bra that covered her breast. The old magic sent flames shooting through her and she clung to him almost desperately, giving back kiss for kiss in a kind of frenzy.

After a time he pushed her away a little and she felt his body trembling as much as her own. 'Cars!' he muttered, slapping his hand down on the steering wheel. 'They design 'em all wrong.'

He took out a packet of cigarettes and held it towards her. When she shook her head he lit one himself. In the tiny lighter-flame she saw the way his hand was shaking. 'I don't, very often,' he said. 'I keep them for emergencies.'

He drew on his cigarette for a while in silence, then he asked, 'Did they give you Christmas dinner at that pub?'

Susan remembered the apples and cheese she had left behind in a paper bag on the dressing table. 'Do you know,' she said in a surprised voice, 'I haven't had anything to eat since breakfast.'

In the dim light she saw Gideon's mouth pull slowly into a grin. 'Do you know,' he replied, 'neither have I.' They both began to laugh immoderately.

There was hardly any traffic on the motorway. As lights and buildings began to appear Gideon said, 'What do you say if we get married as soon as we can get a licence and fix it up? Have you any relatives you want to ask?'

She shook her head sadly. 'No one. My father died

two years ago. He was wonderful. It was he who first taught me to dive, when we lived in Devon. That's why I went back—but it was no good. You can't go back.'

He reached out and put his hand briefly on her knee. 'I'll make it up to you, my love,' he said gruffly.

A little later on he said, 'I've got about three months more in the Caymans—we'll go back to my apartment, shall we, as soon as we're married? Ben is being transferred to the hospital in Grand Cayman next week and he's looking forward to meeting you. And Della and Vic have promised to visit as soon as the Mexican tour is over——'

Susan let him talk on—she didn't care what plans he made so long as they included her.

Charles's flat was in Chelsea, in a tall old house overlooking the river. Inside the building it was warm and silent, the thick carpeting swallowing up their footsteps. The lift took them up to the second floor. At the white-painted door at the end of a corridor Gideon put Susan's case down and fished in his pocket for the key.

He put it in the lock and then looked down at her, standing beside him in her jeans and sensible shoes, the white sweater clinging closely to her, her cheeks flushed and her hair rioting across her shoulders in a pale gold cloud.

He said, 'Charles filled up the fridge when he knew I was coming. There's enough food here to last us until the shops open again. On the other hand——' his eyes looked deep into hers and his brow furrowed '—on the other hand we could probably find somewhere to eat out, and then I could take you back to your bed at the hostel?'

It was a question—he was giving her a choice. And she knew he would do as he said, if that was what she wanted. It would be his way of showing her he loved her and that this was no casual thing, but would last on and on into their future together.

She didn't have to decide. She put her hand over his and together they turned the key and went into the flat, closing the door behind them.

The Mills & Boon Rose is the Rose of Romance

Every month there are ten new titles to choose from — ten new
stories about people falling in love, people you want to read
about, people in exciting, far-away places. Choose Mills & Boon.
It's your way of relaxing:

May's titles are:

THE McIVOR AFFAIR by Margaret Way
How could Marnie kill this feeling of attraction that was growing between her and the hateful Drew McIvor, whom her step-
mother had cheated?

ICE IN HIS VEINS by Carole Mortimer
Jason Earle was a cold, unfeeling man. Yet, given the right
circumstances, Eden could like him altogether too much!

A HAUNTING COMPULSION by Anne Mather
Despite the bitterness Rachel Williams felt about Jaime Shard,
she accepted to spend Christmas with his parents. But Jaime
would be there too . . .

DEVIL'S CAUSEWAY by Mary Wibberley
Why did Maria have to complicate the situation by falling in
love with Brand Cordell, who was angry and bitter about the
whole thing?

AUTUMN IN APRIL by Essie Summers
Gaspard MacQueen hoped Rosamond would come and settle
in New Zealand, but his grandson Matthieu had *quite* another
view of the situation!

THE INTERLOPER by Robyn Donald
It was the hard Dane Fowler whom Meredith really feared. All
the more so, because of her unwilling love for him . . .

BED OF ROSES by Anne Weale
Was her husband Drogo Wolfe's involvement with his 'close
friend' Fiona turning Annis's bed of roses into a bed of thorns?

BEYOND THE LAGOON by Marjorie Lewty
When her deception was discovered Gideon North's opinion of
Susan French would hardly be improved. Why did she care so
much?

SUMMER OF THE RAVEN by Sara Craven
Rowan was stuck with Carne Maitland, the one man she really
wanted — and one who was totally out of reach.

ON THE EDGE OF LOVE by Sheila Strutt
Dulcie fell in love with the cold Jay Maitland — only to find
that his coldness didn't apply to the beautiful Corinne Patterson!

If you have difficulty in obtaining any of these books from your
local paperback retailer, write to:

Mills & Boon Reader Service
P.O. Box 236, Thornton Road, Croydon, Surrey, CR9 3RU.

The Mills & Boon Rose is the Rose of Romance

RAIN OF DIAMONDS *by Anne Weale*
Francesca idolised Caspar Barrington. But she *was* very young
and he did not encourage her feelings for him. Was he right or
was she?

THE LOVING SLAVE *by Margaret Pargeter*
Quentin Hurst was at last beginning to return Gina's interest.
But could she compete with the elegant Blanche Edgar?

THE EVERYWHERE MAN *by Victoria Gordon*
The domineering Quinn Tennant was everywhere! Everywhere
but the one place Alix quickly came to want him: in her
heart.

MADRONA ISLAND *by Elizabeth Graham*
Kelsey Roberts had destroyed Lee's life. Now they had met
again, but how could she extract revenge from a man who
didn't even remember her existence?

SAFARI ENCOUNTER *by Rosemary Carter*
Jenny had to let the forceful Joshua Adams take over her
father's game park. But her real problems began when Joshua
took over her heart as well . . .

WHERE TWO WAYS MEET *by Yvonne Whittal*
The social gap between Margot Huntley and Jordan Merrick
was too wide, and Jordan was only pretending to be
attracted to Margot, wasn't he?

A SEASON FOR CHANGE *by Margaret Way*
Samantha had never met anyone like Nico. He had everything
and he was attracted to her. *So why was she so afraid of him?*

PERSONAL AFFAIR *by Flora Kidd*
Would it make the situation between Carl's cousin Greg and
his fiancée Laura better, if Margret tried to encourage Carl
herself?

LOVE'S AGONY *by Violet Winspear*
Angie had hoped that Rique de Zaldo – now blind – would
love her. But Rique was too bitter to care about any woman . . .

RYAN'S RETURN *by Lynsey Stevens*
The last thing Liv Denison wanted was her husband Ryan
coming back to her. But deep inside her a tiny ember
continued to glow . . .

If you have difficulty in obtaining any of these books from your
local paperback retailer, write to:

Mills & Boon Reader Service
P.O. Box 236, Thornton Road, Croydon, Surrey, CR9 3RU.
Available June 1981

Take romance with you on your holiday.

Holiday time is almost here again. So look out for the special Mills & Boon Holiday Reading Pack.* Four new romances by four favourite authors. Attractive, smart, easy to pack and only £3.00.

*Available from 12th June.

Dakota Dreamin'
Janet Dailey

Devil Lover
Carole Mortimer

Forbidden Flame
Anne Mather

Gold to Remember
Mary Wibberley

Mills & Boon

The rose of romance

Doctor Nurse Romances

, and May's
stories of romantic relationships behind the scenes
of modern medical life are:

ACCIDENT WARD
by Clare Lavenham

When Nurse Joanne Marshall's boyfriend is admitted
to *her* ward, she is pleased to be able to nurse him
herself. But the handsome new registrar, Paul Vincent,
appears and her heart is torn in two . . .

HEAVEN IS GENTLE
by Betty Neels

Sister Eliza Proudfoot takes a job at Professor
Christian van Duyl's clinic and falls in love with him.
But then she finds he is already engaged to a placid
Dutch girl . . .

Order your copies today from your local paperback retailer.

Mills & Boon
Best Seller Romances

The very best of Mills & Boon Romances
brought back for those of you who missed
them when they were first published.

In May
we bring back the following four
great romantic titles.

COUNTRY OF THE FALCON
by Anne Mather

When Alexandra went to the uncivilised regions of the Amazon
to look for her father she was prepared to find life different
from the security of her English home. She certainly didn't
expect, however, to find herself at the mercy of the devastatingly
attractive Declan O'Rourke and to be forced to accompany him
to his mountain retreat at Paradiablo.

FORBIDDEN RAPTURE
by Violet Winspear

When Della Neve went on a Mediterranean cruise, she wasn't
looking for a holiday romance. Her future was already bound to
Marsh Graham, the fiancé to whom she owed everything. But on
board ship she encountered Nicholas di Fioro Franquila, who
treated women as playthings. Was Della an exception?

THE BENEDICT MAN
by Mary Wibberley

Lovely surroundings and a kind and considerate employer —
Beth was delighted at the prospect of her new job in Derbyshire.
But when she arrived at Benedict House she discovered that it
was not the sympathetic Mrs. Thornburn who required her
services as a secretary, but her arrogant and completely unreasonable nephew. Could Beth put up with his insufferable attitude
towards her?

TILL THE END OF TIME
by Lilian Peake

As far as Marisa was concerned Dirk was no longer part of her
life. So it came as a great shock to her when he returned, even
more dictatorial and exasperating than she remembered him,
to disrupt her calm again. Of course, it wasn't as if he meant
anything to her now. Yet why did she find herself wondering
about his relationship with the glamorous Luella?

If you have difficulty in obtaining any of these books through
your local paperback retailer, write to:

Mills & Boon Reader Service
P.O. Box 236, Thornton Road, Croydon, Surrey, CR9 3RU.